S·C·O·U·T

by Julie Nye

Bob Jones University Press, Greenville, South Carolina 29614

Scout

Edited by Suzette Jordan

Cover and illustrations by Stephanie True

© 1987, 1989 by Bob Jones University Press

ISBN 0-89084-413-5
Printed in the United States of America

20   19   18   17   16   15   14   13

Publisher's Note

When Jeff Wingate finds an injured dog washed up on the bank of an island one day, he knows that he is faced with a mystery. But he also finds out what his own limits are. When it seems that he cannot save the dog, he calls on the Lord for help, and God answers his prayer. For Jeff, it is the first step in discovering the two sides of prayer—his own helplessness and God's power. He later comes to realize that his rescue of the dog Scout is one means to teach him to pray for his friends.

The mystery around Scout deepens: how was he injured and where had he come from? And more puzzling, why is nobody looking for this purebred, superbly trained dog? Jeff and his brother Phil seek the answers to their questions, but inside, Jeff is hoping that they'll never find Scout's owner. Now that he has Scout, the two have become inseparable. Strictly a one-person dog, Scout repeatedly shows his loyalty and devotion to his young master. In the end Jeff must wrestle with the question of keeping a dog that is not his, and only then does he realize that he must do what is right.

To Mom and Dad,
whose support made this book possible,
with many thanks for
bringing up their family in
Les Cheneaux

Contents

Chapter One
A Different Sort of Problem

I guess it all started with that boaters-safety certificate. That and the fact that Mom and Dad were in Europe that summer. If Mom and Dad had been home, things probably never would have happened quite the way they did. They probably would have known a quicker way to find the answers, or more likely, would have realized what was going on in the first place, before the damage was done. But then, if it hadn't been for the boaters-safety course, nothing ever would have happened at all.

Now, I know that you may not have boaters-safety courses where you go to school, but, you see, I live in a place where you need boaters-safety before you need driver's ed; so they give us a course on boats and lakes in sixth grade. I'd just finished sixth grade, and the nifty little boaters-safety certificate was hanging in its frame on my bedroom wall. As for where I live, well, that's in Michigan—sure I know you've heard of Michigan, but I'm not talking about Detroit, or Grand Rapids, or any of those places. This is hundreds of miles farther north, in the Upper Peninsula, in a place called the Les Cheneaux Islands.

Les Cheneaux is an area along the south side of the eastern UP. Two towns, Hessel and Cedarville, sit three miles from each other on the shore of Lake Huron. Stretched out between them, on the water, are thirty-six islands—big, tiny, and every size in between. People live on some of them; some of them are government property. A few are connected to the mainland by bridge, but boat is the standard transportation to most.

There are no big cities, factories, or any of the mess that goes with those things. Mostly, there are just small towns along the shores of the northern Great Lakes; hundreds of thousands of acres of forest, still full of deer, bear, and all kinds of wildlife; deep, boggy swamps and marshes; sparkling creeks and rivers, crosscut by beaver dams; and endless miles of beach that alternate flat sand and mazes of huge boulders.

Like I said, there's not much in the way of industry around; most people make their living from tourists in some way or another, and there's sure no shortage of them! They come in droves and masses from all over the United States, even some from Canada. My Dad is sort of an exception to the rule. He's a free-lance writer. He grew up in Cedarville but moved away when he got married. It was a long time before he and Mom were on good enough terms with their bank account to move back. My older brothers and sister, Greg, Phillip, and Karen, who are all in their twenties, had been about my age, twelve, when Mom and Dad bought the house in Hessel where we live now.

Early that spring, Mom had finally convinced Dad that he needed to take her on the super-trip that they'd talked about ever since they were first married; so they decided to combine a long holiday with some research for Dad's writing. The best part of the deal for me was that Phil and his wife Jennifer would be staying with me for the whole summer. Phil is the closest to me in age, and he's only been out of college for a couple of years. He and Jennifer are both schoolteachers, he in math and she in music, but they're pretty neat people anyway—and that's where we get back to the boaters-safety.

See, Dad had told me I could use our little Boston Whaler, the *Luau,* as much as I wanted to that summer. (We have another boat, a big cruiser called the *Regal,* but I figured it would be twenty more years before I was allowed to do anything with her—boaters-safety or no boaters-safety.) Anyway, Phil didn't keep quite as close track of what I was doing as Dad likely would have. Not that I was doing anything wrong, mind you, I was just being—well, you know, expanding my horizons a little bit.

I got to spending more and more time out in the Whaler that first week or so. *Les Cheneaux* is sort of a dialect-corrupted version of the French term for *The Channels,* meaning the varying sized waterways that run up and down between the dozens of islands. I was getting to know their maze like I never had before and even venturing out on open water a little. You have to be awfully careful with a little Whaler and a big lake like Lake Huron, but it can be done, and that's how it happened.

I was out on the far side of Government Island one day. The water is really deep out there, and I was putting along, as close to shore as I dared, scouting for good camping spots. It was way up on the tip of the island, almost to the end, that I saw the dog.

At first, I thought he was dead. Automatically I looked away and turned the Whaler away from the island. I love dogs (we have three), and I can't stand it when I see them by the side of the road after having been hit by a car or something.

Right away, I got mad at myself for being a coward. How did I know if he was dead or not? It was just the way he was lying half in and half out of the water. He never moved as the waves were washing up around him. There wasn't really any beach where he was—just a dirt bank that he had crawled up on.

I knew I had to go back and look. It meant going all the way around the point to get to a rickety old pier—the only one on the island, I think. Once out of the boat, I fought my way through the brush back across the narrow gooseneck of the point. It was tricky to get along the top of the mud bank without getting a dousing, but finally I got down to where I was just above him.

He sure did look dead, but I took a deep breath and slid down the bank toward him. My first thought as I knelt beside him was how big he was. I had thought to just pull him up on the top of the bank, but now I realized that he probably weighed 'most as much as I did.

He was a Doberman—a big one. Black, with perfectly spaced, dark brown markings. I'd only seen one Doberman up close before, but I'd seen a lot of pictures. What caught my eye as he lay there was the twitching in his legs and the faint heaves of his rib cage. A bloody gash ran across the top of his head, another down his

4

shoulder, and a gaping rip in his throat was still gushing blood.

I wish I could tell you how brave I was, but I wasn't. I'd never seen anything like it, and right away, I knew I was going to be sick.

He must have heard me almost choking, because he came awake. As I looked back, I watched him struggle to raise his head. His eyes were open. I spit a couple times and crawled back toward him. Weak as he was, a snarling growl ripped out of his throat.

"Hey, boy . . . easy . . . I'm not going to hurt you. Will you let me help?" I edged up to him. The snarl quieted, and I could see his eyes. They were glassy and dilated. Very slowly I reached out to touch his head. He didn't flinch, but I did. It was sticky and wet with blood. I made myself pull his eyelid down a little. My stomach felt queasy again at what I saw. Instead of healthy red, the inside of his eye was a dull, whitish pink. He was bleeding to death, I realized.

Yanking off my jacket and shirt, I began ripping the shirt into strips. My hands were shaking so badly that I could hardly manage to wrap them around the horrible throat wound. He didn't fight me. Either he'd decided to trust me or he was out again. Just as an extra precaution I tied one strip around his jaws. Even a weak bite from him would have been a noteworthy threat, and I wasn't sure he was going to like what came next.

I'd picked up a length of rope when I left the boat, thinking to put him on a leash or something, if I could. But now, I put my jacket down and worked him onto it, rolling him on his back. I pulled the sleeves up and tied them together with the rope. Then, looping the rope around my shoulders, I tied the other end there too. With a little adjustment I straightened up part way. The dog's weight caught in the rough sling. I waited for him to fight, but he hung like dead weight. He was further gone than I had thought.

Well, it was slow going—trying to half drag-half carry him. The rope bit into my back and shoulders like a piece of baling wire and, pretty soon I could feel the blisters starting to pop up. The brush tore at my face and bare arms until I could feel bleeding there, too. I had to stop and rest about twenty times, and I worried that he might die before I even got him to the boat. I prayed as I went, but I was too tired to think of any words other than "Lord, help!" over and over. But God must have answered my prayers. The dog continued to breathe. I was just about all in by the time I finished the trek to the dock. The old boards creaked and swayed under our combined weights, but I lowered him into the boat as gently as I could, jumped in after him, and covered him up with a blanket from under the back seat.

Then, I sure didn't waste any time. Idling out backwards, I turned around and jammed the throttle down. The little Whaler leaped half out of the water and darted toward the tip of the island. I came around as fast as I dared and pushed the throttle the rest of the way down, heading for the Middle Entrance between Marquette and Little La Salle Island. I was a long way from home, and to a stranger, it would have seemed like I was taking a pretty indirect route, but it was either the way I was going or all the way back to Cedarville Bay and around La Salle Island. The only other possible route would have been around the outside of Marquette

Island, but there are some places you just don't go in a boat like the one I was in.

As directly as I could, I cut across Muscallonge Bay and headed up the channel by the mainland. The process of getting home was like the way one of those little rats runs through a maze looking for a piece of cheese. Up, down, north, south—you can go east only little by little until you're clear of most of the channels and have a pretty much straight shot to the homes east of Hessel, where I live.

The scenery through the channels is breathtaking, but I had no eye for it that day. All I was watching for were the water-skiers so that I wouldn't mow any of them down. I had to slow to a no-wake speed in a couple of spots, but when I hit the last straight-away, I opened the throttle again and kept it there. Speed increased steadily as the *Luau* leveled off in the water. My heart was jamming into my throat as I kept a nervous eye on the speedometer. I'd never had the Whaler wide open before—40, 50, 55 . . . . I tightened my hands on the wheel.

The *Luau* hit a swell, and I think she left the water completely before slamming down again, jarring every bone in my body. I glanced back at the dog, but he hadn't moved. If he didn't have anything broken before, he will now, I thought grimly, but I had other things to worry about. One more smack like that and I'd be lucky to have half my boat left. I tore across the cove to the west of our place, dodging fishing boats and other cruisers. As soon as I came in sight of our house, I began laying on the *Luau*'s horn with long-repeated blasts. I kept that up until I had to have both hands to dock. Still, I misjudged my speed and had to cut the little Whaler in a near complete circle to keep from crashing into the pier. I still bumped pretty hard.

I could see Phil and Jennifer tearing down from the house. All three dogs were already on the dock barking like crazy from the excitement. "Are you hurt, Jeff?" I could hear Phil shouting. "What's wrong?" I was too breathless to answer as I raced to tie the *Luau*. Not till he was beside the boat, with Jennifer right behind him, did he see the dog. He stopped short. Jennifer didn't see the dog—she saw the scratches and bloodstains all over me.

"Jeff!" She jumped right off the dock into the boat. (I'm still not sure exactly what to make of this girl. In some ways she acts like another mother, but my Mom doesn't jump off docks.)

"What happened to you?" She grabbed me and began searching me over for a mortal wound.

"The dog," I finally managed to make a little sense. "He—"

"Did he bite you?" She was horrified as she turned around to see the dog for the first time. Phil was climbing down beside the blanket-wrapped form.

"No!" I shouted hoarsely, tearing away from her. "He's bleeding to death! Phil, can't we take him to the vet?"

"Jeff, where did you find him?" Phil was frowning as he pulled away some of the blankets and bandages. I saw him clench his teeth when he uncovered the throat wound.

"He was over on the tip of Government Island. I thought he'd drowned. Phil, can't we please . . ." I didn't really know what else to say, but Phil was already absorbed in an inspection of the big dog.

"Jeff, go get a tarp out of the *Regal*. A small one." Phil was talking almost absently as he experimented with different ways of putting pressure on the gash. "Jen, go get the car started and put a blanket on the back seat."

I'd scrambled out of the boat before he'd even finished speaking. Soon we had the Doberman in a tarp sling, quite a bit more effective than my jacket had been. With Phil carrying one end and me the other, we made it up the hill and around the house to the car.

I yanked on the shirt that Jennifer had brought me from the house and crouched on the floor beside the dog, who took up most of the back seat.

"Don't get your hopes up, Jeff," Phil said quietly. "I think he's pretty far gone."

He didn't have to tell me. Anyone with one bad eye could see that the big dog was three quarters dead. The vet's initial head shake didn't boost my spirits any, either.

"Pretty slim chances," Dr. Anderson said. Then he shooed us out into the waiting room while he and his assistant went to work. We sat, fidgeting, for over an hour. I kept telling myself that he'd lost too much blood and that he would probably die. But then I remembered that he could just as easily have died during my struggle to get him to the boat. God had answered my prayer and kept him alive. What would Phil say if he knew I wanted to pray for the dog? Aside from teaching math, Phil also taught Bible, and he knew about whether or not you were supposed to pray for pets. I decided not to ask him. I just glanced down and in my head I prayed, "Lord, help!"

Finally Dr. Anderson emerged again, rubbing his eyes and looking disgusted. "Well, he's alive," the big man said grumpily. "That's more than I'd expected."

All three of us broke out in huge grins.

"Don't get optimistic," he continued. "I can't imagine that he'll pull through. I can hardly believe he lasted as long as he did. He's lost an awful lot of blood."

"We'll take it one step at a time," Phil said, still with a relieved grin. "How much do we owe you?"

"I'm paying!" I burst in.

Phil looked around, startled.

"I found him!" I insisted.

Phil's face grew serious, and he glanced at Jennifer. "Jeff, you know he probably belongs to someone."

"I know." I looked away. "But what was he doing way out there in the water? They probably dumped him! Anyway, this was my idea, and I want to pay."

"Where are you going to get the money?" Jennifer asked.

"I have it. I have a lot in my savings account."

Phil's look became even more serious. "Jeff, I hardly think Mom and Dad would okay your withdrawing money for this."

I kept my attention fixed on the magazines on the little table. "I want to pay." After all, I had found him. I had brought him home, and I had even prayed for him.

Phil took a deep breath, then suddenly shook his head. "All right, Dr. Anderson, how do you handle billings?"

The vet sighed wearily, threw up his hands, and said, "All right. Come on back, and I'll have Sharon write you up a charge slip. But I still don't want you to get your hopes up."

We had to leave him there, of course, but Dr. Anderson let me look at him before we left. He was lying in a little three-sided cubicle. I went up close and put my hand on his shoulder. "Hi, dog," I whispered. "Glad to see you made it." The wounds were closed, but the shaved skin all around them was soaked and stained purple with some kind of antiseptic. Multitudes of stitches stood out in long angry-looking rows. An IV needle ran into his front elbow and attached to a clear plastic bottle of fluid hanging nearby.

"Dog," I repeated, stroking his shoulder a little, "you better get tough, y'hear?" His pulse still felt kind of fluttery, I thought, and he didn't open his eyes. Straightening up, I hurried out to the car.

Chapter Two
Discoveries

On the way home, we talked about putting an ad in the paper. It seemed a sure bet though that he didn't belong to anyone local. If anyone in Hessel or Cedarville had owned a dog like that, we'd have known. He's the type of dog that gets noticed.

"Still," Jennifer insisted, "if the owners are looking for him, they'll know to look in the local papers."

"They'd better," Phil commented dryly. "We sure have no idea where he came from, and there are tourists around here from every state in the Union."

I tried to stay out of the conversation. I was already busy hoping that no one would claim him. He sure would be a neat dog to have around. I was sure Mom and Dad would let me keep him. Other kids might have had a problem there, but not me. That's why we already had three dogs. My parents were big softies for strays. Anything—cat, dog, bird, or whatever—that drifted through and had the smarts to look hungry usually wound up with a home.

When we reached home, I went in and changed out of the bloodstained jeans, put my boots on, and took

Cinder for a ride. Cinder is my horse. I guess, while I was on the subject of our family being animal crazy, I should have mentioned that we keep four horses. Cinder is mine, and boy is he a neat horse! He's half Arabian and half quarter horse. That makes him strong, smart, and pretty flashy. He loves to strut and prance. But he has a sprint kick that will just about snap you out of the saddle if you're not careful. He's every bit as big as Dad's quarter horse, Chance. The two other horses are Morgans: Mom's mare, Rela, and her green-broke filly that Mom named Repeat, because she was so much like Rela.

We weren't sure if we were going to keep Repeat or not, but someone was supposed to ride her every day or she'd be a "wild animal" before they got home from Europe, Mom said.

Phil had already had her out that morning, though, and I was glad, 'cause I like Cinder better. He's pretty full of spice himself, and we had a good time charging up and down the beach for a while. There's a good long strip of nice beach that runs east of our property. It belongs to a bunch of different people, but none of them care if we ride across—as long as we don't mow anyone down when we're racing. Normally, it's pretty deserted, though. There are no resorts close by.

I'd been out quite a while before I decided to go over and see Randy. He's my best friend and lives three houses down from us, the other way, west. You can't get down the beach that way. The shoreline goes right up to the woods and it's all swampy. But there's a trail through the woods. You just have to cut across a few driveways and you're all set. So, I took off down there in a hurry. I wanted to catch them before supper and tell him about the dog.

It was worth the effort. He was wildly excited. "You mean a full-blooded Doberman like a police dog?"

"I think so," I hated to admit that I wasn't sure. "He sure looked like it, but he's a lot bigger than I ever thought of a Doberman being. He felt like he weighed a ton."

"Well, you're not exactly Hercules," Randy said giving me a shove. I stumbled into Cinder, who snorted and stepped back, stopping me from retaliating.

"Hey!" I exclaimed. "I can't help it if I'm not chubby—I'm sure taller than you are!" I scrambled aboard Cinder before he could do anything about that. He stood scowling at me. I grinned. Really, Randy isn't even close to chubby. He's just stockier than me. It's sort of like this: if we wrestle, he wins; if we race, I win.

His scowl didn't last but a moment. "Are we gonna go for a ride tomorrow? Early?"

I shook my head. "I don't think any of us are going to ride until later tomorrow. We're going to go back and see the dog first thing in the morning."

"Can I come?"

"I don't know. Probably, if you want to, but I'll have to ask Phil."

"Ask!" he said. "And call me. I want to see that dog!"

"Yeah, well, I want to see him too, but he might not even be alive by then." I hated to even think that, let alone say it, but I knew it was true.

He was alive though, and Phil let Randy go with us. The three of them stood back by the door of the room while I went to the front of the three-sided box where the dog lay. The IV was gone, but he still lay exactly where he'd been the day before. I could feel Dr. Anderson's assistant watching as I reached out and put my hand on the dog's shoulder again.

"Hi, dog," I whispered. To my amazement, his eyes opened. "Hi!" I repeated.

He moved his jaws a little, sort of smacking his lips, but didn't do anything else.

"You're a tough cookie, dog," I told him, moving my hand to the top of his head. "You're going to make it, you know?"

I felt a tremor go through him, as though he were trying to rise but hadn't the strength. A queer, low whine struggled out of his throat. His eyes were rolling around, looking at everything in a funny way. It took me a moment to realize that he was afraid.

"Aw, it's okay, dog," I said, as gently as I could. "You're all right now. Nothing more's going to hurt you. We'll get things straightened out all right. Okay? Yeah, you're okay!" I muttered on, not really knowing what I was saying. That wasn't important, but the sound of my voice was, I knew. Eventually the huge dog sighed a little and closed his eyes again.

"He's very weak." Dr. Anderson's voice came from right beside me. I almost jumped. Where had he come from, I wondered.

"But he'll make it?" My voice sounded funny, even to me.

"Yes, Jeff." Dr. Anderson allowed himself a smile. "I think he'll pull through. I never expected him to even wake up, but it looks like he outguessed me."

Three days later we brought him home. I had brought Candy's leash for him. Dr. Anderson had him in a wire-fenced kennel when we arrived. He sat near the gate, watching alertly as we approached. We'd stopped to see him every day, and Phil claimed he could see the dog gaining strength. He still moved a little stiffly, and you could see a very obvious limp on the leg where the shoulder gash was, but otherwise, he seemed like a different dog from the one I'd hauled off Government Island half-dead at the beginning of the week.

Phil let out a low whistle of admiration as we stopped and gazed at the huge Doberman. Ears perked, he sat motionless. The scars and stitches weren't visible at this distance, and he looked the picture of perfection. His broad chest carried the perfect vest of reddish-brown markings, matched at the bottom of long, straight legs by the patches on his feet. Brown swirled around his throat, crept up the sides of his jaws, and dotted his eyebrows.

As we stopped outside the gate, we could see the lines of stitches on his throat, head, and shoulder, but the purple staining was almost gone. The wounds themselves looked to be healing nicely.

The dog was funny, though. No, not funny—strange. Not a muscle twitched. Nothing moved except his eyes. They darted back and forth from one of us to the other. The day before, he'd obviously recognized me and had been glad to see me. Now I wasn't so sure.

"He's a different one," Dr. Anderson said, as though he'd been reading my thoughts. "Hasn't given me any trouble, but look at him. I'm not sure I'd trust him the distance I could throw him—and you can be sure that wouldn't be very far." He handed me the choke collar that had been on the big dog when I found him.

Phil frowned. "Do you think he's mean? I mean, like a security dog or something? That might explain the situation some."

"No. If he were, we'd have had some excitement with him before now. Those are strictly one- or two-person dogs. Usually pretty much unapproachable by anyone else."

"I'm not sure if I like this idea." Phil turned to me, but I didn't give him a chance to say what I was afraid was coming.

"Oh, come on! Like Dr. Anderson said, if he was going to be mean, he would have been already! He won't hurt anybody!" Even as I spoke, though, I took a quick look toward the still, silent, watchful animal.

"Watch! I'm going to go in and get him!" I moved to the kennel gate.

"Jeff!" Phil's voice was sharp at first. "Okay, but be careful! Move slowly."

Believe me, I did. I opened the gate and slipped inside, careful neither to let it swing shut after me or to move away so that the opening was unblocked. I looped the choke collar together and snapped it to the leash. "Hi, Dog." I spoke clearly and cheerfully. Then, holding the leash and collar forward, "Come! Come here."

To my utter amazement, he did. Not reluctantly or out of curiosity, but quickly. He obviously knew what "come" meant. I stared dumbfounded as he trotted toward me, stopped, and sat facing me. Phil's voice broke my reverie.

"Praise him, Jeff!" he said quickly.

"Good boy! Good dog!" I didn't waste any time either. His jaws opened, and he ran out his long tongue. Shifting a little, he continued to gaze at me expectantly. I reached out to pat him for a moment, and he didn't resist as I slipped the collar over his head.

"Surely he's used to the collar?" I heard Jennifer speaking. "He acts as smart as a whip."

"I'll find out," I said, letting the gate swing shut. "Dog, heel." I stepped forward. Three quick jumps took him around my back to my left side. Again he sat and looked at me.

"Well, I'll be swaggled!" Dr. Anderson was clearly surprised. "Look at him!"

I felt a little foolish as I transferred the leash to my left hand, behind my back. A strong suspicion was growing in my mind that this dog knew a whole lot more about what to do than I did.

He followed me as I walked across the kennel and back, doing militarily precise turns to keep his shoulder exactly even with my knee. I came back to the gate and shrugged in amazement.

"He's awfully well trained," Jennifer remarked. "It's too bad we don't know his name."

"Jeff?" Phil's voice was very quiet. "You know this probably means that he's a really important dog to someone. They're probably hunting high and low for him right now."

Dr. Anderson spoke my thoughts before I had a chance to. "Well, how in the world did he wind up bleeding his way around deserted state property, five miles from the mainland, then, if he's so special? There's nothing on that island but a few camping facilities."

"I don't know, but someone does. Come on, Jeff." Phil opened the gate again. "It's time we got home to do some detective work."

We came. Dr. Anderson began spouting last minute instructions and questions. "You have the salve? The pills? Well, don't forget to keep those stitches clean—and make sure he gets the pill—don't just stick it in his food."

"Okay." Jennifer was laughing. "We've doctored sick animals before. We'll manage!"

Dog leaped into the back seat of the car as though he'd done it a thousand times. He sat there, expectantly watching as I clambered in after him.

The ride home was filled with discussion about Dog. "Maybe he's a police dog," Jennifer suggested.

"Hmm." Phil didn't seem to agree. "The most and the least obvious."

"Why?" That didn't make any sense to me.

"Because that is what he acts and looks like, but if he were, don't you think we'd have heard about it by now? There would have been a huge search."

"Not if they thought he was dead," I reminded him.

"Well, that's easily enough checked on, but I don't think we're going to find it true." Phil was, I knew, mentally already home on the phone. "I think it's more likely that he belonged to some tourists."

"But what about all the wounds?" Now Jennifer sounded skeptical.

"Maybe he fell overboard into the prop on their boat. I don't know," Phil sighed. "I have a feeling it's going to be a long hunt though. If he's the object of any kind of search, we'd have heard about it by now or had a response to one of the ads."

I settled myself back in the seat, hoping that whoever had lost him had given him up as dead long ago.

Chapter Three
Getting Acquainted

Phil did spend a lot of time on the phone, but he didn't have any success. As far as we could find out, the dog had dropped out of the sky in a parachute. No clues as to where he had come from, and no one seemed to be looking for him. Phil seemed a little frustrated, but I was happy.

I spent the days babying him, mostly, and trying to think of a good name for him. Jennifer helped me doctor his stitches and give him the antibiotics. For the time being, we kept him in the laundry room, off the back porch. We didn't want him to have a chance to do too much and break open any stitches or to run away. Plus, we weren't sure how he was going to mix with the other dogs.

The fourth day we had him home, we brought them in one at a time and introduced him to each one. Candy was first. She's a Golden retriever, and a girl; so we didn't look for any problems in them getting along. There weren't, either. Chops was next. She was a real mix-up of a dog. We were never sure just exactly what her ancestry was, but she weighed about six pounds. Just a scrap of dogflesh that always thought she could lick a wildcat.

She took one look at Dog, sitting there by the dryer, and charged him. I didn't think he'd hurt her, but you never know. She attacked his leg with needle-sharp little teeth. He looked down at her, lowered his head and sniffed as if he couldn't believe what he saw, then lifted his foot out of her reach. She made a leap at the dangling paw, then attacked the other one. Dog put the foot back down, sniffed at her again, and sneezed, sending Jennifer and me into gales of laughter.

"I guess she's safe," Jennifer said at last. "Let's try the real test, now."

She meant Reefer, the last of our three dogs. He was a crossbreed, too. Nothing really great to look at, but he was big and heavy. He looked mostly like a Lab. He was even black. But there was a squarishness around his muzzle that wasn't Lab, and his ears stood about halfway up when he got excited. Dad always figured there was some German shepherd in him somewhere.

Reefer was our watchdog, and he took his work really seriously. He was always looking for a fight, and we had to shut him up in the barn when somebody came to visit with another dog. He was pretty much Dad's dog, and he'd been a real grouch for the last couple weeks since Dad had been gone.

Phil brought him in on a leash. I had Dog on the choke leash again, just in case. Reefer took one look and leaped to the end of the lead. Phil held him tight. Reefer had been trying to get into the laundry room for the last four days to roust out the intruder, and he wasn't going to be easily discouraged. He fought

against Phil's hold and growled and snarled, even though his breath was choked off.

Dog had jumped to his feet at the first snarl. His head went down and his hair up, but he didn't growl. I thought that was strange. He didn't even tighten the leash. I gripped it hard anyway, not sure what Reefer was going to do.

Eventually he quit fighting Phil and sat down, discouraged. He was still growling a little. Phil tugged the leash again and cuffed him lightly on the side of the head. "No! You old brawler! You leave him alone, now, understand?"

Reefer knew what that meant, all right. It was just a question of whether or not he would do it. It seemed funny. I'd always thought of Reefer as one of the biggest dogs I knew. He weighed almost ninety pounds, but one glance was all it took to see how much bigger Dog was. As we took our time and little by little they got acquainted and stood beside each other, Dog stood a good four or five inches taller. I mean I knew he was big, but really!

"Well, Reefer, old boy," Phil said, "it looks like you've met your match, hmm?" Reefer didn't like it at all. But he knew better than to try anything now. Phil apparently wasn't fooled.

"I think it's okay to let him out, Jeff, but I wouldn't leave him alone with the beast here for a while anyway."

"I wonder," I thought out loud, "what would happen if they tangled? Not that I really want to know. Reefer's mean, but I have a feeling that Dog would chew him up in little pieces."

"I have the same feeling," Phil responded dryly; "so watch it."

I took Dog out and let him off the lead for the first time. I wondered at first if we hadn't overdone the caution in keeping him confined for so long. He seemed crazy to run, and I couldn't see a bit of stiffness in his shoulder. When he first took off, my heart almost stopped for a moment. I thought he was going to run off. But he went just to the edge of the yard, swung around, and charged back. Straight for me he ran, swerving at the last moment and darting around me. Across the yard to the other side he went, before repeating the maneuver. I stood still and let him run.

He continued doing crazy figure eights around the yard, then began growling and making teasing jumps at me when he came by. It finally dawned on me that he wanted to play. The next time he came by I grabbed him around the neck and shook him as hard as I dared, taking care of the stitches in his throat. A deafening roar exploded in my ear. I let go quickly, startled even as I realized that it was his bark.

Dog jumped away, then dropped to a crouch about ten feet away and ran out his long tongue and panted. I promise you he was laughing at me. "Oh, so you think you're smart?" I approached him slowly, tensed to go after him when he ran. He didn't run. When I had covered about half the distance, he left the ground in a single leap and slammed straight into me. I went down like a felled oak, all the breath knocked out of me.

Dog stood over me for a moment, then began licking my ear when I didn't get right up. "Okay," I gasped, "you win! I give. Just don't do that again."

He seemed to realize that the game was over. I got up and snapped the lead back on his collar. We began a tour of all of Dad's property. It covered about four acres; so it took a little while. We went to the horses, first. I didn't know what Dog would think of them, but he didn't really pay any attention to them. Repeat came over to investigate, nosy snoop that she is. From the way Dog skirted around her and avoided her, I knew that he had been around horses before. That was a relief, because we couldn't have him chasing them. Mom and Dad would have had him off to the pound in less time than it takes to say it. They won't put up with a horse-chasing dog.

We hiked through the woods after that and went down the dividing lines between our property and both neighbors. Dog trotted along as though we were on a policeman's patrol beat. Only when we reached the beach did he hesitate. I let him off the leash again and started out on the dock. Dog stopped when his feet touched the planks. He sat and watched me. I didn't call him but just snapped my fingers.

He flattened his ears in apology and wagged his tail briefly, but he didn't come. "Hey!" I exclaimed, "what's wrong with you? Don't you like water?"

"Of course he doesn't." I just about fell off the dock. Phil's voice surprised me so. I whirled around to see him up on the *Regal's* deck. He chuckled. "You wouldn't like water either, if you'd been through what he has."

Of course! I realized that he hadn't forgotten his experience. But still, I wanted him to be able to go out in the boat with me. "Come on," I said sternly, slapping my leg. "Come!"

He did, but so slowly that I felt bad for making him. He didn't budge an inch from my knee as we went to the end of the pier. I sat down, swinging my feet over the edge. Dog crouched close to my shoulder. "It's okay," I said, petting him and keeping an arm over his back. "You'll get over it. You're not the kind of dog to be afraid of anything."

I didn't have the heart to make him stay out there very long; so I left the dock, went back to the house, and put on my swimming trunks. I thought maybe if I got in the water he'd come too. No deal. I spent a lot of time splashing around in waist-deep water yelling for him, but he just sat on the beach and looked at me.

I gave up and decided to swim out to the rocks that stick up out of the water about a hundred feet from the end of our dock. They're what we always use for markers when we're having races or something. This time I only got about halfway out though, before I heard somebody yelling my name from the beach. "Jeff, hey, Jeff!"

I turned partway around and treaded water until I could see that it was Randy. When I joined him on the beach, Dog celebrated his delight to have me back by jumping around and running in circles, acting like a nut again.

"Whyn'cha tell me you were going to take him out?"

"I didn't know I was. We just decided to, I guess." I tried to dodge the frolicking animal. I wasn't very successful—he kept spraying me with sand. As wet as I was, it stuck to me like glue.

"How's he acting? Have he and Reefer tangled yet?"

"No, they haven't. But I have a feeling they're going to the first time our backs are turned. Reefer hates him."

"That's going to be a terror of a dogfight." Randy didn't sound enthusiastic.

"Yeah, tell me about it."

"What's he doing? Is he crazy or did you feed him catnip?" Randy dodged as Dog made one of his mad charges by, inches away.

"I think he's just happy to be loose. He was doing this before." I couldn't restrain a grin as Dog circled around Randy, leaped up, and let loose one of the trumpeting barks right in his ear. Randy jumped.

"Crazy dog!" he grumbled. "What have you been doing with him?"

"Right now, I was trying to get him to go in the water. I guess he connects the water with getting torn up, or something. He won't set a foot in it."

"Just like your Mom the year that they found that twenty-foot snake over in the Straits." Randy snickered.

"Yeah." I had to grin, too, at that memory. The Coast Guard or somebody had found this monstrous snake over towards the Mackinac Bridge. It was twenty miles from us, but Mom didn't go in the water for the rest of the summer. "I don't think it's that bad. He'll get over it. He's been acting really smart about everything else. We walked around the property. Phil said to do it. Sort of let him know where our boundaries are and let him scout around some. That way, maybe—" I stopped and looked at Dog, puzzled. He'd broken off his race and swerved to sit in front of me just like he always did when I called him or whistled.

"What's the matter, Dog?" I asked him. "What do you want?"

"He acts like he thinks you called him," Randy said, with an equally puzzled frown. "That's what he did before."

"I know," I said, "but I didn't. All I said was, well, I don't know. What was I saying?"

"About Phil wanting you to show him around the property. To let him scout some—" That did it. Both of us knew right away. As Randy said the word *scout,* Dog's head turned briefly toward him before he returned his attention to me.

"Scout!" I cried delightedly. "That's his name!" My excitement knew no bounds. "Scout! Hey, Scout!" The big dog went wild with his own excitement. He just about wagged his stub tail right off. He leaped up and grabbed my arm in his huge jaws. I pulled but couldn't pull it loose. He backed away and forced me halfway down in the sand. I was laughing so hard that I could hardly resist anyway. I don't know if he was excited to hear his name again or if he was just excited because I was. By the time he let go, I could have qualified for Tar-Baby, if they'd have excused a little extra grit.

"What in the world is going on?" I heard Phil coming up off the dock. Randy replied, explaining how we had just discovered the Doberman's name.

"Scout, huh?" Phil sounded just as pleased as we'd been. "Really? Hey, Scout! Come here! Scout!"

Scout reluctantly moved away from me and went toward Phil. "Sure enough," Phil responded. "That's the first time he's obeyed me when you were with him. Well, you old tramp," Phil roughed up the dog's ears, "I guess if you're going to hang around, it's just as well that we know what your name is. I'd sure give a lot to know some more about you, though."

I wasn't particularly sure that I wanted to know anymore. The more we knew, the greater the chances were that someone was going to show up and claim him. The more we learned about Scout though, the more it stuck out like a sore thumb that someone had put an incredible amount of time into training him. It was hard to believe that anyone who would take that much trouble with a dog—someone with that much know-how in the first place—wouldn't be combing the world looking for him.

Later that evening, we were all sitting in the den after supper. Phil was buried in the evening paper, and I was completely involved in the latest adventures of the Jell City Gang. With my nose in the book, I almost missed it. Phil silently kicked the bottom of my foot. I looked up, and he indicated Scout, lying on the rug at my feet.

He had been sprawled out full length, but now he was up in a sitting position. His ears were cocked fully upright, and all his attention was focused toward the kitchen—or the door. I couldn't tell for sure. A low growl came from him; then he barked softly. Just once. Quickly he glanced up at me, then returned his attention the other way.

I looked at Phil and shrugged. "What's the matter? What's he hear?"

"Beats me." Phil sounded no more sure than I did. But just that moment we heard a car crunching over the gravel driveway. At the same moment, we heard Reefer thunder his usual challenge as he came charging up from the beach.

"There's your answer." Jennifer shook her head in amazement. "He heard someone coming. Good ears on that boy."

Phil shook his head in amazement. "Somebody is missing that dog," he said, getting up to go to the door. The visitors were Mr. and Mrs. Keller and Randy. We often sat with the Kellers at church, and it wasn't unusual for them to drop in during the week and vice-versa. But they hadn't been over since Mom and Dad had left for Europe.

"We've been hearing so much about this dog," Mr. Keller said, "that we thought as long as we were out, we'd stop by and see him."

"There he is." Phil indicated Scout, still sitting beside me. "Come on in and have a seat."

Scout, apparently realizing that the Kellers had been admitted to the house, flopped back on the rug and lost all interest in them. They stayed for a couple hours. We wound up playing Uno, but most of the conversation was about Scout and how we might be able to find out who had lost him. But by the time Kellers left, we were no closer to a solution than we'd been the first day.

Like I said before, I really wasn't straining my mind to try to think of any new ideas.

Chapter Four
Smart Dog

The next day was Sunday; so I didn't have a lot of time to spend with Scout. Especially since we had company over for dinner. By the time we got home from the morning service, ate, visited, and cleaned up, it was practically time to go back for the evening service. I didn't mind though. I like Sundays. Especially during the summer. It seems like it gets to be an awfully long time between my visits with some of my friends. We don't exactly live right in the middle of town, and some of them live a lot farther out.

Of course, Phil always made it a point to talk with me about the sermon on the way home, to make sure I'd listened. Phil had a lot of hopes for me—I was getting old enough to see that. I guess with a beautiful island to live on, horses, and boats, he might have worried that life at Les Cheneaux was too easy. That was why, in spite of his protests, he'd let me pay for Scout's treatment. Probably, I thought, he would have been pleased to know I had prayed for Scout. I decided to tell him about it when we talked about the sermon.

The service that night was especially good, because Phil and Jennifer did the special music right before the sermon. Phil has a nice voice, I guess, but Jennifer's is something else. She was a music major in college. More piano than singing, I've been told, but she certainly does have a beautiful voice. This was the first time most of the people in church had heard her sing.

I looked around while they were in the middle of the first verse. I really love our church. There's absolutely nothing fancy about it, and it's not very big. But everything's finished and furnished in a real light, golden color of varnish: the walls, the pews, the pulpit, the piano. In the summer, the doors at the rear and the front of the auditorium are usually left open to keep it cool so that the flags on the platform wave and snap in the evening breeze. The sun was beginning to slant, and the fiery rays made the building glow as though everything in the room was reflecting gold.

I glanced out the window as Jennifer started the second verse as a solo. The church was situated high up on a hill, and below me I could just barely see Lake Huron over the treetops. The blue water sparkled like millions of diamonds in the late sunlight. Jennifer's beautiful voice filled the auditorium:

> In the strength of the Lord let me labor and pray,
> Let me watch as a winner of souls;
> That bright stars may be mine in the glorious day,
> When His praise like the sea billows rolls.

Phil's baritone joined her.

> Will there be any stars, any stars in my crown,
> When at ev'ning the sun goeth down?
> When I wake with the blest in the mansion of rest,
> Will there be any stars in my crown?

I don't know where the crazy old thought came from, but all of a sudden I missed my parents so badly that it was almost a physical pain. I shoved that out of my mind quickly enough to smile at Phil and Jennifer when they rejoined me a few minutes later.

When we got home, Phil decided that he and Jennifer were going to go for a walk. (We live so far north, that in the summer, it really doesn't get dark till around ten o'clock.) They asked if I wanted to go, but I hadn't had a chance to finish my book before Kellers had come in last night; so I curled up in one of the chaise lounges on the deck and applied myself to the end of the mystery.

I did finish and was sitting there staring out over the water, slapping at mosquitoes, and making plans for the next day when the phone rang. I scrambled out of the chair, almost tripping over Scout, who was, as usual, lying beside my seat. "Hello?" I said into the receiver, a little breathlessly.

"Is this the Wingate residence?" an official-sounding voice asked.

"Yes," I replied. My heart did a double flip-flop. Scout! I thought. Someone saw the ad. . . .

But the voice was continuing, "Please hold for a three-party call from Alan and Elizabeth Wingate." I almost yelled out loud. Mom and Dad!

The few seconds before they came on the line seemed like an eternity. Finally I heard Dad's voice. "Hello?"

"Dad!" I did yell this time. I was so glad to hear him. A deep chuckle answered me.

"Easy on my ears, Jeff. We can hear you."

"Mom, are you there, too?"

"Yes, honey. I'm here. How are you?"

"Fine! Where are you?"

"Salzburg."

"Where?"

"Salzburg, Austria. We're going to have thousands of pictures for you when we get back. But tell us how things are going there." Mom sounded typically concerned. "Is Phillip being good to you?"

"Yeah, um, I think there's something you ought to know, ah. . . . "

"What?" Dad broke in.

"I wish Phil was here," I said. "He and Jennifer wanted to tell you, I think, but they're out walking somewhere."

"What?" Dad asked, a little louder.

"Well, Dad, we have another dog—at least for a while." I launched into an abbreviated account of finding Scout and what we had gone through with him so far. I made it as short as I could, conscious of an intercontinental phone bill, but they kept interrupting me with questions. When I finally finished, they were both quiet for a moment.

"The poor thing." Mom sounded almost indignant. I grinned. I told you she was a big softie. Dad was too, really, but he just didn't show it so much.

"You are making a good effort to locate his owner?" Dad sounded concerned.

"Yeah, Phil has called about a hundred people and run more ads than you could count, but no one's heard of him. Hey—" I interrupted myself. "I bet—hey, Dad, can you guys hang on for just a second? I'm going to see if he'll go get Phil."

"Come on, Jeff. He's not that well trained, is he?"

"I don't know, but I wouldn't be surprised." I set the phone on the table and snapped my fingers at Scout.

He followed me to the door. I thought hard for a second, then grabbed Phil's jacket off the coat stand by the door. I bunched it up and stuffed it against the end of Scout's nose.

"Find him!" I ordered. "Find. Search. Get him." I tried to think of every word that might be used as a command for something like this. Scout pulled his nose away from the coat and looked at me. I tapped it with my hand and put it back for a moment. "Find Phil!" I opened the door and pointed out. "Go on. Go find him!" Scout gave me one last glance and bounded out. He disappeared off the deck in about three jumps.

I jumped back for the phone. "Well, he's going somewhere," I told them. "I don't know if he'll get them or not." For the next few minutes they brought me up to date on where they'd been traveling and what they'd been seeing. The traveling sounded interesting enough, but Mom was talking about all the art galleries and museums, and that sounded like a first-class bore to me.

It must have been at least another ten minutes before I heard Phil's voice shouting up to me from the beach. "Jeff! Jeff! Is something wrong?"

I interrupted Mom's account of Paris. "Phil's back! Just a second. I'll go tell him you're on the phone. He's down by the dock, I think." I put the phone down again and ran to the door. Throwing it open, I yelled as loud as I could.

"Hurry up! Mom and Dad are on the phone." I didn't wait for an answer but rushed back to the phone to say my goodbyes. I knew that once he got inside, I was going to lose my place on the line. It wasn't but a moment, either, before Phil burst in the door with a big grin.

Jennifer and Scout were right behind him, even more breathless than he was. I relinquished the phone to him, and Jennifer ran for the upstairs extension.

Scout looked from one of us to the other, bewildered. Suddenly I realized that he must have understood what I'd asked of him. "Good dog!" I exclaimed enthusiastically. "Good Scout! You're a smart one, aren't you?" He knew it, I guess, but he just about turned himself inside out to show his appreciation for the praise. He wiggled and squirmed when I patted him and thumped him in the ribs.

Phil and Jennifer talked for a while. I could tell from hearing one end of the conversation that they were discussing Scout again. I felt better about the whole thing now that Dad knew. It seemed like it was more official that I was going to get to keep him.

"Yes, sir," I kept telling Scout. "You're a smart mutt, you know that?"

When the long conversation finally ended, Phil confirmed that Scout had indeed come looking for him. "Scared me to death," he said. "We were down by McGregor's, and all of a sudden here comes Scout, about sixty miles an hour, barking and whining, jumping at me and running back toward the house. I didn't know whether someone was hurt or whether the house was burning down."

I grinned again. "Well, he got you here, didn't he?"

"Hmmph." Phil was trying to sound irritated, but I knew he wasn't really mad. He was glad that he'd gotten to talk to Mom and Dad, too.

I glanced at the clock on the wall. It was nearly ten thirty. I decided to take Scout out for a last run before getting to bed. We were all going to go out for an early morning ride; so I needed to get moving.

It was a beautiful night. I could see why Phil and Jennifer had wanted to take a walk. The tide was up and the waves were crashing high on the beach. A gentle breeze was blowing from the west, swirling up the damp, clean musk from the swampy forest. There was cedar mixed in it, and spruce. A million stars glittered in the velvet black sky above me. They seemed close enough to reach out and touch. I located both dippers and the North Star and wondered what the stars looked like from Salzburg.

Somewhere in the trees up by the house a whip-poorwill began his chanting repetition. I stood, facing out across the water, and watching Lake Huron churn and recede at my feet over and over and felt sorry for all the people in the world who don't live in Les Cheneaux. It's at times like that when I get to wondering about things that went on in the past. Dad expected us to be pretty familiar with the history of our hometown, and I knew that although Sault Ste. Marie, about forty miles from us, was the oldest settlement in Michigan, the ground I was sitting on had been one of the last parts of the United States to be settled. When the rest of the country was celebrating its Bicentennial, Les Cheneaux still had eight years to go before its Centennial. This had still been Indians' territory when the Civil War was over and done with.

I wondered what it must have been like a hundred years ago or more. Who might have been standing on this very spot, watching the waves roll in? A Chippewa Indian? A French trapper with a pack full of furs, having beached his canoe for the night? A Jesuit missionary, scouting for new converts?

Mom always tells me that I'm going to be a writer like Dad. She says I'm a dreamer, but I don't think that's all that bad. I think she might be right, though. One thing I know I'd like to do is know more about some of the people that used to live in these waters. Mom is always reciting a poem that Longfellow wrote about the Upper Peninsula: "The Song of Hiawatha." I'll admit that I'm not a big fan of poetry, but that one's always talking about "the glory of the sunset and the purple mists of evening." I don't know much about Longfellow, but it sounds like he knew about Les Cheneaux.

Scout finished his romp and came back to me. I noticed that he didn't come close to the water though. Oh, well. That was going to be tomorrow afternoon's project: coaxing him into the Whaler for a ride. If he was going to live here, he was jolly well going to have to get used to the lake.

I turned and started back up toward the house. Its bright lights stood out in contrast to the smudgy, dark background of the trees surrounding it. I glanced down at the big dog pacing beside me and wondered if the people who settled this area had had the help of dogs as good as him.

Chapter Five
A New Complication

The morning sun came up red and hot. We were out riding before it made its appearance over the tip of Marquette Island, but the heavy, humid air along with the scorching heat carried the promise of a storm. Thunderstorms in the islands are regular occurrences, and they can be frighteningly wild. They come boiling in across the channels, shaking the ground, flooding the swamps, soaking the beaches, indiscriminately frying the big trees, and hurling lightning against the water with sufficient force to be heard three counties away. Fortunately, tornados are not part of the package. In all the recorded history of Les Cheneaux, there's only been one tornado that touched down anywhere near, and that was a long time ago.

This morning, though, we could tell that it would be a while before we had to worry about the big white thunderheads that were piling up in the northwest. In fact the sky where we were was clear and blue, and the early morning air was still crisp. Randy had shown up in time to ride with us; so I let him take Cinder.

That left me with Repeat, but Jennifer liked Rela and Phil wanted to take Chance.

Riding Repeat was a little like tobogganing on a really steep hill: fun in its own way, but you just sort of take off and hope for the best. You never know for sure, though, what's going to happen or what condition you're going to be in by the end of the trip.

Phil's a better rider than I am, and he usually took her, but he wanted to get on Chance again; so he claimed it would do me good to ride her. Maybe. At least it's never dull. I have my own theory about Repeat. I think that she has a phobia of keeping her feet in the same place for more than a second. They're never still. Every second from the time you cinch her saddle till you pull it off, she's dancing around. She'll stop, if you make her—that is, she'll stop moving forward. But she'll basically jog in place until you let her go again.

So by the time we had been out an hour, I was tired. Cinder considered an hour's ride a nice warm-up for the real thing. He was still trying to coax any of the other three horses into a race. Phil kept telling Randy to hold on to him and make him stay back until we got out on the beach.

The beach was always our standard race course. The horses knew it, too; so when we approached the sand about a mile above our property, all four were prancing and chewing their bits. We let them go. The results of a charge like this were pretty well cut and dried before we ever started. Chance has the fastest jump—he's trained as a working stock horse. But Cinder is the hands-down winner in a straight race. After the first few leaps he's in front and gone. Dad always says he could outdrag a stock car. He has all the quarter horse drive and sprint, but the Arabian in him seems to quintuple the distance that he can hold it. We've matched him against a lot of horses, and when most of them—no matter how fast— are using up the last of their sprinting power, Cinder is still winding up. Repeat and Rela aren't exactly slow, but Morgans are just not generally as speedy as some other breeds. Plus, Repeat hasn't fully mastered running full out with someone on her back. Mom says the weight unbalances her. I don't know, but you do have to watch her, or she'll stumble on you in mid-stride. You can't do anything cute like jumping her over a drift log or dodging back and forth quickly. She'll miss her lead change and dump you faster than you can say Jack Robinson.

This race had a new element, however, that none of us were used to: Scout. He had been some distance behind us in the woods when we started the charge down the beach. I was last of the four, trying to keep Repeat content just to follow Rela along, when I saw Scout angling out from the trees. He was apparently determined not to be left behind. I thought he would be anyway. Horses are fast—a lot faster than dogs, unless you're talking about a greyhound. But as I was beginning to learn, Scout seemed like the exception to a lot of rules.

The big dog headed straight toward Cinder, who was taking the lead. He leveled out, close to the sand, his long legs nothing but a blur. He didn't appear to be running so much as flying low. I'm sure my mouth dropped open a foot as I watched him cut down the gap between himself and the sprinting bay gelding. Chance shied violently as Scout shot by him, almost depositing Phil into the bay.

"Hey!" he shouted at Scout. "Watch it, you big thug!" But as we pulled the horses up, I realized that he too was amazed at the Doberman's speed.

"I never thought any dog could run like that," he frowned in amazement as he stared down at Scout who was panting happily, wondering if we were going to repeat the fun.

"There's sure a lot I'd love to know about him," Jennifer said in her quiet way. "He is definitely no ordinary dog."

That was for sure.

We walked the horses in to cool them out, then went in and ate breakfast like we hadn't seen food in weeks. Jennifer thought Randy and I were so funny. She never had any brothers, and I guess she wasn't used to how hungry guys can get. She made French toast by the pile and fried up a bunch of venison sausage. That was Phil's and my favorite breakfast. No matter how much she made, there was never any left over. The French toast was made out of fresh, homemade sourdough bread, and we flooded it with tons of maple syrup, made from the sap of the hardwood trees about five miles north of our place.

Once finished, we helped her clean up some; then I was ready to head for the boat. I wanted to get in a good cruise before there was any hint of rain. The channels are not the place to be during a storm. I always figured there were a whole lot of easier and less dangerous ways to scare yourself, if that's what you were bent on doing.

I asked Randy if he wanted to come, but he had a dentist appointment and had to go home. I whistled to Scout and we set off. He started sulking as soon as we reached the dock. I had to order him to heel before he reluctantly came out to the end where the Whaler was tied. It was a five-minute project to get him into the boat. I didn't want to put a leash on him and try to force him, mainly because I wasn't sure I could. I knew he weighed more than I did.

Eventually, he was sitting in the bottom of the Whaler, pressed against my knee as I started the engine. When I got up to untie, he just crouched down on the floor. I felt bad, but I really thought he would get over it. It took a while, but after over an hour of putting around Hessel Bay, he seemed to be perking up some. I kept telling him to "Watch" something, or "Look at that, Scout! Look! Look!" I would put all the excitement into my voice that I could. I think it finally began to occur to him that he wasn't going to get banged over the head or half drowned again, because before long he was up in the passenger's seat beside me, staring out over the broad, flat front of the boat, ears flying back, and tongue hanging out.

I couldn't help laughing. "You're no coward, Scout," I said with relief. "You're just smart enough not to make the same mistake twice, if you can help it." I was glad to know that I'd been right—a dog who loved to ride in the car as much as he apparently did could learn that a boat was even more fun. I was willing to say that within a few days, he would be begging to get in every time we were on the beach.

I was getting a little bored with the scenery where we were; so I went out around Club Point and opened up the throttle most of the way down the long channel. I took my time after that, and we aimlessly wandered out through Cedarville Bay. You have to watch out for

SCOUT

a lot of water-skiers over there, though, especially during the big tourist season; so we cut our speed down even more and drifted out toward the open water through Boise Channel.

The beautiful colors of the islands never fail to impress me, no matter how many hundreds of times I see them. The water is so blue that it makes anything else you've ever called "blue" seem like a joke. The sky is almost the same vivid tint, but not as dark. All around you, in irregular, weaving patterns, the varying greens of the wooded islands rise and fall from high bluffs to flat stretches that are underscored by streaks of white sand. There aren't many houses out here, unlike back towards town. Most of this land is state property, and the only breaks in the green color are the rusty splashes of the tamarack trees.

The thunderheads were piled up halfway across the sky by now, and the rising wind was already kicking up some whitecaps. I kept an eye to the west as I pulled around Government Island and began putting up the far side. I scanned the shoreline with interest, remembering how I had found Scout farther up toward the point. How in the world had he gotten out here, I wondered. I looked to my right, across the vast stretch of unbroken waves. Lake Huron stretched before me— hundreds of miles of her. Not many passenger boats come through here, except for the big cruisers that make their runs up from Detroit and Port Huron.

They don't habitually shed Doberman pinschers as they pass by, though. I let the *Luau* creep in closer to the shoreline. I never had determined if there were any good camping spots out here on this side. The water runs really deep, right up close to shore, out here. There's

48

almost no beach. There was, however, one place where it leveled out. It wasn't exactly a beach. More like a flat spot that the waves washed over a little bit.

I was about to turn the Whaler back away from the island when I heard a low whine from Scout. He was standing with his front paws up against the side of the boat. His attention was fixed somewhere on the shoreline, less than fifty feet away.

"What's the matter, boy?" I strained my eyes, but I didn't see anything unusual. The wind was blowing off the island toward us; so I thought maybe he'd scented an animal of some sort. Squinting against the sun that was reflecting off the water in dazzling rays, I scanned up and down the shoreline again. Nothing.

He let loose another whine, louder this time. It crescendoed and almost turned into a bark. I looked over at him, just in time to see him bunch his muscles and hurl himself over the side in a magnificent leap that carried him fifteen feet from the boat.

"Scout!" I yelled after him, but he either didn't hear me or ignored me. He surfaced and started swimming for the island. There was nothing I could do but watch. I didn't dare take the *Luau* any closer.

Scout reached the shore in a surprisingly short time. He couldn't get up on the bank in the first spot he tried. He turned parallel to the bank and started down toward the flat spot. When he reached it, he scrambled up, shook himself once, and bounded toward a tangle of driftwood. As soon as I saw where he was headed, I saw the little patch of red among the branches that lay there.

"What is it?" I wondered aloud as I watched Scout dive on it and pick it up. Dogs can't see red—they're color blind! How in the world did he even know it was there? More to the point, why should he care?

He turned and came out to the edge, by the water, again, the red thing held in his mouth. He put it down and began barking like a crazy dog. He grabbed it up, dropped it, and dashed ten feet down the shore and back—then started barking again. He kept this up until the echoes of his barks were resounding back from the islands all over the West Entrance. I yelled at him a couple times, but I guess he was making too much noise to hear me.

Finally, he stopped and lay down in an alert-looking crouch, watching me. I could tell, because his ears were pointed straight toward me. I cut the *Luau's* motor and called to him again. He stood up and kept looking at me. In spite of the fact that my ears were ringing from the comparative quiet, I could hear him whining. I stuck a couple fingers in my mouth and gave a whistle that they could probably hear back in Cedarville Bay.

"Scout!" I yelled again. "Come!" I put all the authority into my voice that I could. There was no way I could get to him without going all the way around the other side of the island.

Once again, he surprised me. Without any further hesitation, he picked up the red object and jumped off the bank into the water. It took him a little longer to get back to the boat than it had to get to shore, because he was going against the current. When he got close, I moved around to the back of the boat where it sat lower in the water. I wasn't sure if I would be able to pull him up over the side.

He came to where I was, after repeated urging, and, I grabbed his collar. He got a foothold somewhere and was into the boat before I could even decide how to try to get him up. He shook water all over me, of course; then he put the red thing down again and started the barking routine all over.

I don't know if you've ever been in a Boston Whaler or not, but if you haven't, let me tell you that there's not much room for a hundred-pound Doberman in the first place—particularly not one who's jumping on you, barking, and bounding all over the place. I was almost mad.

"Knock it off, Scout! You're crazy!" He quit but continued to whine and quiver with excitement as he forced himself to stay in a sitting position.

I leaned over and picked up the red thing that he had retrieved. It didn't look like anything special to me. It was at least twelve inches long and bigger around than I could reach with the fingers of one hand. It seemed to be made out of foam rubber—squishy and soft, but the exterior was tougher than that. I had seen Dad use this type of thing before when he was field-training a bird dog. "Dummies" they call them. But this wasn't quite like that.

There was also a little indentation on the side, with a bar that was part of the tube itself, in the side. Sort of like something that you would hook something else to. I held it up in my hand and looked at Scout. He crouched eagerly, watching me, as though he expected some kind of command. He was obviously so pleased with himself that I figured he must have some connection with the thing.

I sat down. Scout edged up and put his head on my knee. "Dog," I said thoughtfully, rubbing his ears, "you're a weird one."

He groaned in pleasure and stuck his nose next to the red tube.

I thought that maybe it was some kind of a training device that he had been taught with. It was surely obvious enough that somebody had spent a lot of time working with him. But how in the world could he have spotted it from the boat? It wasn't that big, and dogs have pretty poor eyesight anyway. I held it up to my nose, but it didn't smell like anything. Of course, a dog has better smelling ability than a human, but still—!

The *Luau* was drifting dangerously close to the shoreline; so I started her up and headed back for town. Scout curled up contentedly on the floor, the tube tucked between his paws.

When I showed it to Phil, he didn't know what to make of it, either. "Do you suppose we should turn it in to the police?" he mused as he looked at it.

"No." I didn't think it was anything that important. "Look." I took it from him. "You can tell that there's nothing in it." I bent it almost double. "I think it's like one of those little dummies that Dad used to use to train the Labs with."

"Yeah, could be. It's about the right size. And if it floats, I guess it would work for something like that. Oh well, I guess it really doesn't matter. The police have already said that they haven't lost any dogs." Phil grinned. "Besides, he's not even tattooed with an ID number—and those kind of dogs always are so that they're not sold to some scientific experimenting company."

I guess that was one of those things that Phil had found out while he was making all the phone calls about Scout. Anyway, we showed it to Jennifer, too, and among the three of us, we decided just to forget it. It didn't seem like anything to get excited about. Scout seemed to disagree, though.

For the rest of the day he carried it around with him. That night, he took it upstairs to my room.

The storm hadn't really hit yet, though it had been raining most of the evening. As I was getting ready for bed, though, I could hear gusts of wind start to toss the big spruce trees around outside my open window. I cut off the light and went to the cushioned window seat. I knelt there, watching the storm move in. Scout came and stood beside me, all his attention fixed outside too.

The distant rumblings of thunder grew stronger, and I could see the lightning flashes now. All of a sudden a bluish flame shot straight down to the water, about two hundred feet offshore. The sizzling crack was deafening and closely followed by a roar of thunder that shook the very foundations of the house.

I looked at Scout to see how he might be taking this. Some dogs come unglued during these storms. He just stood, staring out the window like he was as interested as I was.

The rain came harder. Torrents of it poured down on the house and the water. The solid, colorless curtain shut off what little view I had in the blackness of the night. Only the rapid, blinding flashes of lightning allowed me to see the *Luau* and the *Regal* down by the dock, being tossed around like toys, straining against the ropes that held them.

I watched until the storm began to slacken, then crawled into bed. I left the curtains open so that the fresh, cool cleanness of the rain-washed air would fill the room. I fell asleep, lulled by the pouring rain on the roof above me.

Chapter Six
What a Mess!

When I got up the next morning, Phil was already sitting out on the front deck with Scout. The dog sat facing him as he held the red tube in his hands. He was lightly tossing it back and forth from hand to hand and moving it up and down slowly. Scout followed the motions with his eyes and faint tilts of his head, as though he were watching a meaty bone.

"Hi," Phil greeted me without ever taking his eyes off the dog. "This animal is something else. Look at him."

"He likes it, that's all." I shrugged and flopped into the lounge. "He's not acting any dumber than Reefer when you hold a stick."

"No, I know, but there's something more, Jeff. I'm tempted to cut this thing apart and see if there's something we're missing. I mean, it feels like plain old foam rubber, but—"

"Phil." I sat up and stared at him. "Give it to the poor dog. You're driving him crazy."

Phil looked at me, startled, then at Scout. The big dog's attention hadn't wavered. His big brown eyes were fixed on the tube in mute appeal.

"Okay, okay." Phil laughed and flipped it to him. "You're probably right." Scout caught it neatly. Going to the corner, he lay down, cradled the tube between his paws, and put his chin across it with a huge sigh of contentment.

Shaking his head, Phil turned back to me. "You look like you're dressed for a ride."

"Yeah, Randy's coming over and we're going to go out."

"You're not going to let him try Repeat like he said he wanted to?"

"No. She'd kill him."

"Who are you taking, then?"

"Doesn't matter, I guess. Do you want me to leave Chance for you?"

Phil thought for a minute. "No, you guys go ahead and take him. That way Jen and I can take Rela and Repeat. The filly will probably behave better with just the two of them, anyway."

"All right." I stood up as I saw Randy coming out of the woods trail. "See ya. We're going up towards Search Bay."

"Okay—hey, Jeff!" I stopped on the steps and looked back.

"Hmm?"

"Keep an eye out for the new family up by Peterson's. Jen talked to the wife the other day, and they have a son somewhere around your age. I guess he really hasn't met anybody yet. They have horses though, I'm told; so maybe you'll have somebody new to ride with."

"Okay." I was willing enough. I always liked meeting new people. I was all the way down the steps before I realized that Scout was beside me. He had even forsaken his precious tube.

"So you're coming, huh?" He looked up at me and wagged his stub tail. "Okay, if you want to." I patted his head and ran to meet Randy.

Cinder and Chance weren't particularly eager to be caught, but eventually we were under way. You can't always ride straight up the beach, even when you get beyond Randy's place. There are rocks some places where the waves crash up five to ten feet high, and other places the water goes right to the trees. But there are trails that criss-cross around and cut in and out of the woods. We stay on the beach when we can, because it's easy riding and because you can talk better when you're side by side. Scout bounded along. He dashed around, investigating all over the place, but at no time was he any further than fifty feet away.

It wasn't until we came out on the last stretch of beach at the top of the bay that we saw the other horse and rider coming toward us. Even at that distance we could tell that this was probably our new neighbor. But neither of us was paying much attention to the rider. Randy let loose a low whistle of admiration as he stared at the flashy horse approaching us.

I'd never been a big fan of Appaloosas, but I had to admit that this was an unusually beautiful horse. He was about Cinder's height, but a little lighter in build. A solid, true black covered him from nose tip to flank, where a thick blanket of gleaming white spots began. They ran over his hindquarters, perfectly spaced, and down his back legs, leaving a jet black tail in their midst.

He looked like the kind of horse you see in show magazines.

Only when they got right up to us could I drag my attention back to the boy on his back. "Hi," I said, a little weakly. "You must be part of the new family— and boy is your horse gorgeous."

He didn't look very friendly, but he replied, "Yeah, I'm Mike Denal."

"I'm Jeff Wingate. We live out on the point. And this is my neighbor, Randy. I think he likes your horse, too." I had to smile at Randy, who hadn't yet taken his eyes off the Appaloosa.

"Well, Casper's pretty special." Mike smoothed the inky black mane. "He's a lot sharper than regular old quarter horses." He flicked a disdainful glance at Chance and Cinder.

My blood pressure shot up about five notches right there. I had to bite my tongue to keep from saying the sharp retort that came to mind. What in the world did I say that made him mad? I wondered.

I saw a couple of spots of red coming into Randy's cheeks too, but he snickered and said, "Casper? Like in Casper the Friendly Ghost?"

"No, stupid. Casper as in Wyoming. He was bred there and named for it—or don't you guys know anything about the way good horses are dealt with?" The sneer on the older boy's face continued to puzzle me, even as it made me so angry I couldn't keep myself from answering.

"My horse has a pedigree longer than both your arms!" I knew my temper was shredding, but I didn't care too much all of a sudden. I hardly noticed Scout standing beside Cinder, looking from me to the stranger with rapt attention. "He has the best points of quarter horses and Arabians, and they're breeds—not colors!"

"Huh!" Mike was getting more hostile. "Shows what you know. Casper's from racing stock."

Randy's hoot of laughter interrupted him. "Hah! Cinder can outrun anything in Mackinac County!"

"I don't think he can." Mike's smugness made me want to hit him. "You've just never seen a horse run, that's all."

I set my teeth and looked away. What was this guy's problem? We hadn't done anything to him—we'd never even seen him before. But I knew about another sixty seconds of this was going to make me hate him.

"C'mon," the older boy goaded, "let's see. I'll race you around to the other side."

I looked up at him, meeting his eyes directly. "It's your funeral, chum." Actually, I didn't know if Cinder would beat the Appaloosa or not. The black and white horse looked light and awfully fit. He moved on his feet with the grace of a dancer.

But I've never in my life turned down a race.

"All right," I continued. I knew the distance around the bay was just about perfect for Cinder. A little less than half a mile.

"I'll count," Randy said, his excitement showing in his voice. "Then I'll follow."

I expected he would, will or no. Chance wasn't a great deal slower than Cinder, and he wasn't big on being left out of a race.

We turned Cinder and Casper shoulder to shoulder. I felt Cinder tense. He knew what was coming. So did I. As he bunched his hindquarters, I locked the heel of my hand under the saddle horn.

"On the count of five." Randy was enjoying himself. He was more confident than I was. "One, two, three, four—"

I don't know whether or not it was deliberate, but Casper shot away as Randy said four. Cinder immediately leaped after him, giving me good reason for my grip on the horn, but the Appaloosa had the lead.

He wasn't more than a few feet ahead though; so the sand was flying in our faces. Mike swung the ends of his long reins to the left side, where we were, toward Casper's rump.

Cinder didn't like that, and he slowed. "Giddup!" I stood in my stirrups and slapped his shoulder. "Hiyah! Cinder, go! Go! Go!" I yelled in rhythm as his driving strides lengthened. I could feel him leveling out, and I knew his tail would be cocking up, as it always does when he really gets moving.

I swung him a little further left to clear Mike's swinging reins so that we were charging through about four inches of water. But Cinder was used to that. We rounded the top curve of the beach neck and neck. I could hear Mike yelling, but I did nothing more. I couldn't stop Cinder now if I wanted to.

I could feel the big bay straining more and more. Sheets of water splashed up as high as his back as we came around the final part of the curve and moved up on the sand again. With firmer sand under his hooves, Cinder's rocketing pace increased even more. Finally, he pushed his nose in front and passed Casper smoothly. I let him go until we were a few lengths in front, then pulled him down. I turned back to see Casper stopped also. I wasn't sure if Mike had pulled him in or if he

had quit. He was blowing hard. Cinder snorted once, and breathed rapidly but easily. Arabians have incredible endurance.

Really, I knew the Appaloosa had done well to hang on so well. They're from quarter horse stock and don't usually do so well at longer distances.

I started back toward them. The strip of beach we were on was pretty narrow, and all of a sudden a pheasant, probably disturbed by our commotion, flew out of the woods with a thunder of wings. Both horses shied—even Chance, who was still approaching, reared and spun away.

I'm not sure exactly how it happened, but Mike wound up sprawled in the sand. I jumped off Cinder to grab Casper's reigns before he could take off. I had my hands pretty full with them, but I could see Mike, red-faced and obviously angry, pick himself up and come toward me. Cinder was dancing away and he pulled me away from Mike. The next thing I knew I was sprawling in the sand myself, after a rough shove from behind.

"Get away from my horse!" I heard Mike's voice. "You ignorant, backwoods—"

I rolled to my feet and lunged at him. I wanted to hurt him. I'd never been so mad at anyone in my life. It didn't even matter that he was so much bigger than me that he'd probably kill me. If I got in one good punch before I died, I figured it would be worth it. We tangled but good. I'm not sure who got in the most hits, but it lasted about five seconds.

A hard, black body tore between us like a canine rocket. Scout sent us both flying in opposite directions. His snarls and yelling barks stood my hair on end as

I struggled to get up again. "Scout, no!" I yelled, spitting out a mouthful of gritty sand. The big dog had already made another leap at Mike, but he stopped the mad rush and his teeth clicked shut inches from Mike's bare arm. The rest of his jacket and shirt hung in tattered shreds from his shoulder.

Scout didn't move away, though. He stood over Mike, snarling like a caged wildcat. He meant business, too. His head was low, legs stiff, every tooth exposed, and ears flat against his head. I'd never known what was meant before by the term "blood-curdling" growl.

Very slowly, I got up and went to him. I wasn't sure what he'd do.

"Scout," I put my hand on his collar and got a good grip. "Come!" I pulled back as I spoke. Reluctantly, but immediately, he followed me away with no resistance. "Down," I told him. He dropped in the sand but kept a watchful eye on Mike.

I leaned over and put my hands on my knees. I felt winded and sick to my stomach, and I could feel my lip swelling rapidly. From the way it was throbbing, I suspected I was going to have a black eye, too.

I made myself look up at Mike. His face was still pasty-white, and he looked quickly away. Both of us knew that our fighting moods were long gone. I didn't need a second look to see that his nose was bleeding badly.

Randy rode up. "I'm gonna go get the horses," he said quietly. I glanced up the beach where Cinder and Casper were unconcernedly nibbling at the bushes and nodded.

When he left, I knew I had to say something. I was going to have some tall explaining to do when I got home, but more than that, there was a big sense of shame growing in me every minute. I had hardly done a thing right from the start. Mike had started out unfriendly, but I knew I had fueled the fire.

I had no idea what do next, but I knew I had to make an attempt to fix this. I'd messed up—bad.

"Mike," I burst out suddenly, "I'm sorry. I really am."

He scrambled to his feet abruptly. Scout started, perking up his ears, but he didn't get up.

"I'm gonna have your dog shot," he said thickly. "You and your—"

"You are not!" I could feel my face flush again. "You started it, and he was just trying to protect me! Wait, please!" I tried to keep him from interrupting me.

"I really am sorry for making such a bad start. We ought to try to be friends. There aren't many guys out here our age."

"Get lost," he muttered, turning away.

"At least, let's not hate each other!"

He swung to face me suspiciously. "You're weird."

Suddenly I fought a grin. "You're not exactly normal yourself."

He didn't smile, but he didn't turn away. His nose had stopped bleeding. He went to the water, scooped some up, and rinsed his face.

"Sorry about your shirt," I said. "What's your Mom going to say?"

"Nothing, if she doesn't see it," he said abruptly. I was surprised.

"Aren't you going to tell her?"

"I'll just get in trouble." He wasn't facing me; so I couldn't see his expression. "What are you gonna tell your folks? You can't hide your face very well."

"The truth, I guess." I shrugged. "What choice do I have? Except it'll be my brother. My parents are away for the summer."

"You get me in trouble, and I'll blacken your other eye." The belligerence was coming back.

"I'm not going to get you in trouble—but I'll have to tell them if they ask."

"My Dad will knock the tar out of me if he finds out. Then I'll fix you good."

I sighed. Apparently there was no reasoning with this guy. I could hear Randy coming up with the horses. I changed the subject and gave one last try at patching things up.

"Mike? Why not come riding with us sometime? Civilized-like, I mean. There are some places over by—"

"Maybe." He cut me off. Grabbing Casper's reins, he vaulted into the saddle. "But don't count on it." He booted the Appaloosa into a run, and they were gone.

Randy and I stood silently for a moment, before he broke the silence. "What a jerk."

"Hmmph." I couldn't think of anything to say.

"Man, I thought he was a goner. Scout would have killed him, I think."

I turned away and climbed on Cinder.

"What's Phil gonna say?" Randy's chatter went unchecked.

"Plenty, I'm sure," I said. "But right now I'm willing to risk it for an ice pack. I can hardly see out of this eye. Let's go." He mounted, and with Scout following dutifully, we set off for home.

Chapter Seven
The New Neighbors

It seemed to take forever, but finally we reached home and had the horses taken care of and put away. I kind of hoped Randy would just go home, but he tagged along as I started for the house. I knew he'd get all mad at me if I asked him to leave, and I just didn't feel in the mood for arguing with anyone.

We hadn't taken two steps inside the kitchen when Jennifer spotted me. She was in the middle of cutting up the lunch salad, and she just stopped, knife in one hand, tomato in the other, and stared at me. I braced myself, but to my surprise, she kind of smiled, as though she were trying not to laugh. "Who stepped across whose line?"

I didn't think that was very funny, but Randy snickered. Jennifer pushed the salad back on the counter, wiped her hands off, and came over to me. "Well, let me see—do you still have an eye under all that?"

I stood still and let her inspect me. In a couple more minutes, she had out the ice, antiseptic, water, and all that kind of stuff. I gritted my teeth while she cleaned up everything the best she could. She never did ask any questions though. One time Randy started to say something, but I stretched my foot under the table and kicked him. Hard. I guess he got the message, because he was quiet after that.

Jennifer was almost done when I heard Phil clumping up the front steps to the deck. "Jennifer!" He called as he came in the front door. "We're in luck. There's fresh perch for supper! They're biting like—"

He broke off abruptly as he came through the archway and saw me. The silence grew awfully loud, and I could feel the tension level climbing by the second. Unlike Jennifer, he didn't laugh. He came over to the table and leaned his elbows on the back of the chair across from me.

"What in the world have you been up to?"

I knew better than to try to dodge his questions. The best I could hope for was that he wouldn't tell Dad. "I guess," I started uncomfortably, "that you could say I met one of our new neighbors."

Phil's eyebrows shot up. "Jeffrey Robert Wingate, are you telling me that you got in a fight with the guy from the new family—the first time you met him?"

Randy could restrain himself no longer. "The other guy—Mike—he tied into him, Phil!" Randy was bubbling in his eagerness to contribute. "He nailed Jeff from behind before he could even—"

"Be quiet, Randy!" I almost yelled. "He's not asking you!"

"Jeff!" Phil straightened up and took a step toward me. "You don't talk to anyone like that! Now you tell me fast and straight what went on out there!"

I tried. At least Randy didn't interrupt again as I did my best to tell him exactly what had happened from the time we first spotted the Appaloosa and his rider till he left us. When I finished, Phil continued to stare at me for a long, long moment; then he sort of collapsed into a chair. He leaned his head on his hand, and I could tell he was thinking.

"I think you're going to have to go up there and apologize to him and his parents, Jeff."

Randy spoke up again. "From the way he talked, Phil, I don't think that's going to do Mike much good."

"Well, our problem is not Mike. Our problem is what we need to do. Among other things, I think we need to discuss this as a family, Randy, which means I think you better scoot home."

"Okay." Randy sighed and slid off his chair. I didn't even turn around to say goodbye as he went slowly out the door, letting it bang behind him.

"Did you realize that part of what I meant when I talked to you this morning was that the Denals are not a Christian family, Jeff?"

I squirmed a little in my chair. "No, not really, but I guess I know that he didn't act like a Christian."

"Neither did you." Phil's voice was very pointed. "I realize that he was hard to get along with, but who would have been able to tell from your behavior today that you were a Christian?"

I was having my own personal staredown with the tablecloth, feeling the shame well up in me again. "I did tell him I was sorry."

"Did you tell him why? Specifically, I mean?"

I shook my head.

"You're going to need to find a way to show Mike that the Lord is more a part of your life than what you've demonstrated today."

SCOUT

It was awfully quiet in the kitchen for a while. Jennifer started putting lunch on the table. I watched her setting out slices of ham and cheese, along with the sourdough bread and fresh salad. My empty stomach twisted inside me. I wished Phil would be a little more specific about what he wanted me to do so that we could get on with lunch—before my lip was so swollen that I wouldn't be able to eat.

I didn't have long to wait, but not for what I thought. We heard Scout, sitting outside on the back deck, give the one, single bark that we'd grown used to hearing by now. We knew what to expect, and sure enough, Reefer followed up with his own series of challenges to the car we heard approaching.

Phil got up and went to the door to see, but somehow I didn't need to be told. I heard Jennifer go to join him, and I heard her speak first. "Well, hello, Mrs. Denal. It's so nice to see you again."

The screen door opened and shut behind them. "This must be your husband, and. . . . " The voices faded to murmurings as they moved farther from the door. I sat still. I had no desire to get up and face any of them. My head still throbbed like an overgrown toothache. I wondered if they would really try to have Scout condemned as vicious. It didn't seem possible that they could—he'd just been doing what almost any dog would have done. It was just that Scout was Scout, and he seemed to have his own methods for accomplishing anything.

The voices came closer again, and I heard Phil talking. "Come on in. He's in the kitchen." I closed my eyes briefly and took a deep breath. As they all trooped in, I stood up and turned around to face them.

"Oh, my word!" That was the lady that must have been Mrs. Denal. She was tall and dark and rather pretty. Her husband was right behind her. He was tall and blonde and looked kind of mad. I knew I must have looked a sight, but the expression on Mrs. Denal's face told me that it was probably worse than I had thought.

"Jeff," Phil came about halfway to me. "These are Mike's parents, Mr. and Mrs. Denal."

"How do you do?" I said, a little hesitantly, taking a quick look at Phil for a cue to how I was supposed to be acting. He didn't give me one; so I took the plunge on my own. "I'm awfully sorry about what happened today. I was really wrong and—"

"We came over here," Mr. Denal interrupted me, "because Mike has something he would like to say to you." He stepped aside so that I could see that Mike had come in behind them. He sure didn't look like he wanted to say anything, but he stepped forward and muttered something that sounded like an apology.

"Let's just forget it, Mike, okay?" I was squirming with embarrassment about this whole situation. "We'll get along fine—there aren't too many people around here to ride with; so we'll have a chance to get to know each other better."

"Yeah." He didn't sound very excited about the idea. Then Phil and Jennifer were urging the Denals to stay for lunch. I wasn't very excited about that idea, but no one asked my opinion. They accepted, eventually, and the adults did most of the talking during the meal.

That was fine with me. I didn't have a whole lot to say. I did keep my ears tuned to the conversation though, when I heard it start turning to Scout.

"Word seems to be getting around town about him." Mr. Denal apparently liked Scout. "Even though I'd never seen him before, I had a fellow ask me about him while I was in town the other day. I guess he overheard me talking to the postmaster about how the mail was delivered out here. So this guy came up and asked me if I lived out by Point Brulee. When I said yes, he asked me if I knew the people who had found the Doberman. I said no, but he asked a lot more questions about whether or not you'd been able to track down the owners."

"That's funny," Phil said. "We haven't really told that many people. I mean, there've been a lot of ads in the papers and such, but we haven't done a lot of talking about it."

"Well, he sure was curious." Mr. Denal finished off his iced tea. "Are you sure he's not some sort of police or military dog? He sure looks like he could be, and from what you tell me of his actions, it seems likely."

"We thought so too." Jennifer took over the explanations for a while and outlined the search we'd gone through so far trying to locate Scout's owner. I lost track of what she was saying. My head was pounding so badly that all I wanted to do was go upstairs and lie down. I realized I probably wasn't being a very good host to Mike, but every time I moved my head it hurt— and that sure didn't make me feel like talking.

Jennifer was still talking when Reefer, Candy, and Chops, who were all still outside, set up an incredible racket. We could hear them tearing around the house and running for the beach. Scout gave a low growl and trotted through to the front door.

"Oh, no!" Phil and I moaned together. When they do that, it usually means one thing . . . there's a guy up the beach a way that has a huge hunting dog. It's some kind of hound, I guess, but not a purebred. He comes down here every now and then, and Reefer hates him. There's always a big fight, and Reefer usually just about gets his ears chewed off before we can break it up.

We both scrambled away from the table and ran for the front door. Sure enough, Chops and Candy stood a safe distance up the hill toward the house, barking encouragement, while Reefer tore towards a big black and tan hound down on the beach.

"Reefer!" Phil bellowed, but he might as well have saved his breath. As it was, he rushed toward the dogs, frantically looking around for a big enough stick to make an impression on them. Enough noisy commotion was coming up the hill to account for about six dogfights.

Reefer sailed into the other dog, who had stood, quietly waiting in anticipation. There weren't many dogs that Reefer couldn't lick, but this was one of them and the hound knew it. Bandit (I knew his name from hearing Dad plead with his owner to keep the dog home) loved to work out on Reefer. I think that's why he came down so much. Maybe he put it in the same category as some guys do a quick workout at the gym.

Events took an unexpected turn this time. I almost didn't realize it when Scout left my side with a single, soaring leap that took him over the edge of the deck to the lawn six feet below. Scout completed his flight down the hill in less time than it took me to get worried about what he was going to do. He charged up to the pair of rolling, tumbling animals and took a hand—

or maybe I should say a jaw. About five seconds later, Bandit was stretched out on the ground between Reefer and Scout, screaming like he was dying. I guess it was a good thing that Phil had gone down.

I collected my surprised wits enough to whistle for Scout. He let go immediately, and Phil grabbed Reefer. Bandit came up like a jack-in-the-box. I guess he wasn't hurt too badly, because he could still run. He took off down the beach toward his home, ki-yiing like a whipped puppy. We could hear his yelling getting fainter and fainter. He wasn't wasting any time about getting home.

The moment of silence that followed was broken by Mr. Denal's shout of laughter. It scared me so badly that I almost jumped off the deck, too. I hadn't realized they were all standing right behind me. I turned around and was surprised to see that even Mike was grinning.

"What a dog!" Mr. Denal was almost beyond control. "You sure you don't want to get rid of him, Jeff?"

"No, sir!" I said. I think he might have said more, but Jennifer spoke softly.

"Well, would you look at that?"

Below us, on the lawn, Phil was making his way back to the house. Reefer and Scout had been following, sort of. Now, they stood, shoulder to shoulder. Both of them were really tense, and they were sniffing at each other. I thought they were going to get into a fight of their own, but all of a sudden, Scout gave a really short, sharp bark and jumped away. Reefer jumped after him, and almost before I could realize what was happening, Scout was tearing away in one of his big circles of the lawn, just like he always did when he was trying to get me to play.

Reefer chased him, but he might as well have tried to catch a deer. Scout stopped though, and let Reefer slam into him. They both went rolling around on the ground, and this time it was Reefer who jumped up and charged away.

We all stood and watched, dumbfounded, as the two big dogs romped around the yard. They must have worn each other out quickly, because pretty soon they stopped and stood panting, one tail and one stub wagging.

I shook my head in disbelief. Reefer never wagged his tail at other dogs—not even at Candy. Phil continued to stand on the lawn and stare at them. Finally he turned and came up on the deck.

"I have now seen everything," he remarked. "The world holds no more surprises."

"Didn't they like each other before?" Mike asked him.

"No, all they ever wanted to do was fight each other."

"Hmmph." Mike didn't say anything more. I didn't miss Phil's long stare in my direction. I finally had to look back and meet his eyes. He raised an eyebrow and glanced toward Mike. I knew what he was saying, even though he wasn't saying it. What a drag—to get shown up by your own dog.

There was a bit more laughing and talking about the scene we'd just watched; then the Denals left. They said that they had company of their own coming for dinner; so they'd better get going.

Nothing personal against them, but I was glad to see them go. The minute the door shut behind them I was downing a couple of aspirin. I didn't wait any longer before making my way upstairs to lie down. Scout followed me, of course, and from my bed I watched him curl up on the rug and lick unconcernedly at a chewed-looking spot on his side.

"Dog," I said, "you're something else."

It wasn't until the next day that Phil brought it up again. "I know he's hard to get along with, Jeff, but if you look at it from his point of view, he's a solitary stranger who felt like he had to prove something to you and Randy. He knows he doesn't fit in here yet, and it irritates him. That might be one reason he's so gruff."

I didn't answer. At least he hadn't told me that he was going to tell Dad. Apparently, though, he wasn't finished. "Mr. Denal told me that Mike really resents having to move here."

"Why? Where are they from?"

"California. I guess Mike is really good in athletics, and everybody was looking for him to do outstanding things this year—he was supposed to start high school in the city where they'd always lived. He thinks they're living in Timbuktu now and doesn't see many advantages to it. He's made up his mind that he is not going to like any part of it or any people that go with it."

"That's dumb."

"How would you like it if Mom and Dad moved away from here to Chicago, or something like that? Do you think your attitude would be perfect?"

That idea shed a little new light on the subject. I thought anyone who wouldn't want to live around here would be crazy as a loon, but maybe Mike thought that way about California, too.

"It would be good if you could show him that not everything here is dull and boring."

"How am I supposed to do that? He won't even talk to me."

"You'll think of something. And I think you might help the situation by praying for Mike. You told me yourself that you prayed for Scout when Scout needed help. If God answered those prayers for a dog, He won't forget prayers for Mike." Phil smiled. "Just keep a watch on your temper. You've got a lot of bad impressions to undo, I'm sure, as far as Mike is concerned."

"Yeah, I guess." I thought about it for a while. Looking at it from his point of view, maybe Mike's hostility was understandable—a long way from justified, I thought, but understandable.

Chapter Eight
Practice Time

When I sat down to breakfast the next morning, Phil was reading a letter. He responded to my "Good morning" with a grunt; so I gave my attention to the scrambled eggs. Jennifer was already washing dishes. I realized that I was getting a little careless about sleeping late. I had barely got a good start eating when Phil decided it was time to share the letter with me.

"Jeff?" I looked at him and saw a glint in his eye.

"Yeah?"

"Know what this is?"

That was a pretty dumb question. "No." But I could tell he liked it, whatever it was.

"Well, are you feeling in the mood for a few workouts this week?"

I just frowned. I wasn't sure how to take that. It could have been dangerous to say yes, depending on what he had in mind.

"There's going to be a special speed contest over in Moran this weekend. Not run like the normal ones. This is going to be a special fund raiser for the Red Cross. I didn't know about it before."

I was interested. In case you don't know what "speed contest" means, it's sort of like racing competition with horses, except you're not just racing. You're going around barrels and poles and in and out of patterns and all kinds of crazy things. There are a few events that are standard, like the barrel race, the pole bending, and the keyhole, but beyond that, speed contests can be a lot different from each other. Sometimes you never know what you're getting into until you're actually there, but they're always fun. There's a local organization called the Tri-County Speed Association that holds a lot of contests; plus there are 4-H competitions, and stuff like that, but this was something a little different.

"When do we leave?" I couldn't suppress a grin. We usually show quite a bit during the summer, but Dad had put the brakes on this year, just because he couldn't be here to supervise. This had been Phil's idea, though— I sure wasn't going to do anything to veto it.

"Well, the competition is all day Saturday, but we're going to have some practice to do before then."

"Yeah." I realized that this was going to be no picnic, really. "The horses haven't been worked much at all this summer."

"They're in good shape, though," Phil commented, "as much as we've been riding. And Chance won't need much brush-up. He's a pro."

That was true. Chance was trained within an inch of his life as a working cow horse. There wasn't much he wouldn't do, if you could get the idea across to him. Cinder was another story. He was fast, all right, but he tended to get real excitable around race time. If you were going to have to be dragging him out of a run

really quickly, you'd best do a little weightlift
beforehand. Phil was rattling on, though.

"There's going to be all the usual, of course. Even
the Indian pick-up. Plus, I guess there's going to be
some sort of a timed obstacle course that they call a
free-for-all. What d'ya think? Do you want to try it?"

"What is it?"

"Oh, all kinds of stuff—all timed of course, but you
have to do it with a partner, switch horses, open and
shut gates, and just about everything they can think
of."

"Well, if I'm still alive after Indian pick-up, I guess
it wouldn't hurt to try. I haven't grown more than a
couple inches since last time Dad and I were out there,
and then I think I was missing as often as I made the
jump." Indian pick-up is this deal where you have one
guy on the horse and the other standing at the far end
of the ring. The horse runs down to the other end; you
pick up the second rider behind the first and run back.
It sounds a lot easier than it is, because if you're going
to make any kind of good time, you have to make the
mount while the horse is still running—or at least not
fully stopped. Randy hadn't yet been able to compete
here. He just wasn't able to make it up before the horse
took off again. I'd only been doing it for two years.

"Practice makes perfect." Phil was always optimistic
about this kind of thing. "Let's get out there after
breakfast, then, and see what those beasts remember
how to do."

We'd been right about Chance. We had him and
Cinder in the big field behind the barn, and it didn't
take him ten minutes to catch on to the idea that there
was a contest coming up. He dropped his ho-hum

a worn-out coat and started paying real
n to what was being asked of him.

wound up, as usual, and I had to strain
patience with him, making him repeat steps
over and over again until he listened to me. Probably
the most critical thing in a speed contest is making sure
your horse is on the right lead at the right time. By
that, I mean that when they're running, either their left
or right front foot is reaching the furthest ahead on
each stride. That same foot is sort of the last one on
the ground before they take another stride. It carries
their weight while they turn. So if they're turning to
the right, they need to be on the right lead. To the left—
left lead. If not, then at best they'll be off balance and
not as fast as they could be. At worst, they'll fall.

The tricky part comes with things like barrel racing
and pole bending, where you're going one way one
second, and the other the next. The horse has to pay
attention to you when you tell him to switch. Cinder
tends to be a little sloppy about picking up his right
lead; so you really have to watch him or you'll wind
up in the dirt.

Chance is a dream to ride in stuff like that. You
hardly have to cue him, even. He knows probably more
than I do about the best moment to switch. His time
is hardly ever better than Cinder's though, because
Cinder can make up on the straight-away what Chance
gains on the turns.

The pick-up was what we worked on the most. Phil's
great at that. He and Greg, my next-oldest brother, used
to do it all the time, with each other and with Dad.
If you can place your horse anywhere within five feet

82

of him, he has a hold of the horn and he's up behind you before you can hardly think about it.

Now, me—that's something else altogether. The idea is that, when the person on the horse gets close to you (assuming you're standing facing him), he'll run the horse just barely to your left. The second he reaches you he'll "put on the brakes" to double the horse back—around the outside of you—toward the finish line. Anyway, as he comes by you, you grab for the saddle horn with your left hand and get a hammer-lock. Some people prefer to lock wrists with the person in the saddle, but whatever's easiest for you, you do. Then you have to make a vaulting jump up behind the rider. Ideally, your other hand goes on the back of the saddle to help you swing up, but with me, my other hand grabs whatever's handy: the blanket, Phil's shirt, the horse. . . .

Really, if the horse doesn't have to slow down too much to wait for you to grab on, the momentum will almost yank you right up there by itself. You just have to watch out not to get kicked on the way up. If you miss, it's legal for the person in the saddle to hold on to you, if he can. When I did this with Dad last summer, we had been known to make the return trip across the arena in some pretty squirrelly positions, such as me with one leg across the back of the horse and one under his belly, head about level with Dad's hip, while his elbow was locked around my neck, or else me lying belly-down across Chance's rump, Dad hanging onto my boots with one hand, while I hung on for dear life to one of his on the other side. Needless to say, we didn't place with these circus routines, but we sure gave the spectators some laughs.

All the time we were in the field practicing, Scout sat over under a little maple tree, watching. A couple of times when we stopped to let the horses rest, I spoke to him. He just fixed a very bored eye on me, as though to ask when we were going to do something interesting.

"You'll get your fun, kid," I told him. "We'll take him with us, won't we, Phil?"

"I don't know, Jeff. Do you think it would be a good idea to have him there around all the people?"

"He never misbehaves!" I didn't see any sense in that argument. "If anything, it'll make jolly-well sure that nobody messes with the horses while we're having lunch or something."

"Well, maybe." Phil still looked skeptical. "There'll be a lot of people there, too. Maybe someone who knows something about him will spot him."

That wasn't exactly what I'd had in mind, but I decided it would be wisest to let the last comment go. "Come on." I remounted Cinder. "Let's try this thing one more time—then I've had it! I'm ready for a swim."

We kept at it for the next three days. We really should have been working on it for a lot longer time, but like I said, we hadn't really planned to do much in the way of competition this year.

Cinder settled down some after a while. He learns to pay attention to you too, but just not as quickly as Chance. We experimented with different ways of getting me up more efficiently during Indian pick-up, and little by little, improved our time.

Jennifer came out to watch a couple times. She had never ridden in a contest. I thought it was a shame, because she's really pretty good, and ladies compete too—although some of the events have separate divisions. One afternoon when we finished our practice, we plodded slowly back to the side of the field and found Jennifer and Scout sound asleep under the little maple tree. Scout was snoring loudly.

"Some cheering squad you are!" Phil exclaimed, kicking the bottom of Jennifer's shoe lightly.

"Hmm?" She rolled over and looked up at us groggily. "Oh, hi. Finished already?"

"Already!" I snorted and led Cinder off to the barn. Scout stretched lazily and trailed along. "Don't you look so innocent, either," I grumbled at him. "We work while you rest, then you insult us by snoring at our performance."

I didn't really mind, though. I would have loved to go through this for the competition even if not a single person cheered for us. It was fun. We let the horses rest on Friday and spent most of the day cleaning up our tack and trailer, inspecting everything for loose or faulty buckles or weakened straps.

I talked to Scout a lot that day, explaining to him what would be going on during the contest. "You're going to have to keep an eye on things," I told him. "You never know what's going to happen at these contests." Boy, I didn't even realize what I was saying.

Chapter Nine
The Competition

We thought that we'd made an early start, but by the time we turned the last corner and came in sight of the big, sloping roof of the grandstand, we could tell that the old fairgrounds was already a busy place. There's nothing fancy about the Moran facilities. I guess once upon a time it was (and looked) new. But now, it's just a big grandstand and track, with the open area in the middle marked off in a couple of arenas. There are some buildings off to the sides—the kitchen and the exhibit hall—and most everything looks like it needs a coat of paint.

Mostly, though, we didn't pay any attention to that. Our attention was all on finding a place to park the trailer in the midst of the ones that were already lined up around the field on the outside of the track. Finally, we succeeded. Piling out, we began to unload the horses. We'd only brought Chance and Cinder, of course. Rela just wasn't the kind of horse you used in competition like this. She was sweet tempered and docile—more of a pet than anything else. Mom would have murdered us if we'd ever riled her up by teaching her to run barrels and poles.

When we had the horses tied out on the shady side of the trailer and sprayed with fly repellent, Randy and I went exploring. We wanted to find out who the competition was and exactly what was going to be going on during the day. Phil took off in the opposite direction toward the exhibit hall, which was serving as the registration building today.

We hiked around among the trailers for a while, exchanging greetings with people we knew and evaluating the horses of those we didn't. We didn't see anything unusual or unexpected until we reached the far side of the field. I was still scanning the trailers to one side, trying to see if the Denals had showed up yet. I knew they were coming, and I wanted to find out what events Mike was going to enter Casper in. It never hurts to know where your competition is going to be, you know.

"Toledo." Randy's voice brought my gaze around in a hurry. He wasn't excited or anything. He sounded more stunned. "Would you look at that?" When I spotted what he was watching, I felt a little stunned myself.

Rod Ketler's trailer stood a few yards to our left. I recognized it, and I recognized Sniper, the chestnut quarter horse standing beside it. But there was another horse beside Sniper. I found myself staring in amazement, wondering how an animal like that had found its way to our community.

I'd seen thoroughbred racing horses before, but only on TV. It didn't take much figuring out that I was looking at a live one now, though. He was a dark, slate gray that almost turned to a black around his head and legs.

Tall and long legged, he shifted around constantly on his tether as though he were nervous. He was lightly built, with long, sloping shoulders and a deep chest. His barrel tapered up to a set of hindquarters that looked awfully light to me, but I realized that I was used to the build of a quarter horse. This horse's muscles were flat and lean, like the long tail that hung behind him and the neck that had very little arch to it.

It didn't take a professional eye to see that he was a runner, though. He might as well have had "speed" spray-painted on his side.

"Toledo!" Randy repeated with a little more feeling this time. "Do you suppose he belongs to Rod?"

"Yep!" The voice right behind us made us both jump. We spun around to face the tall, grinning young man behind us.

"You wouldn't believe what I had to go through to get that horse, but he's all mine now, and I'm going to clean up!"

"He's a thoroughbred, isn't he?" I asked.

"Sure is. He's got a pedigree as long as your arm, an official Jockey Club tattoo number on his lip, and a really weird name—'Just Charge.' Stable guys called him Cricket, though; so I do too."

We stayed long enough to find out that Rod had him entered in the half-mile race, the Indian pick-up, and the free-for-all. The race didn't bother me. Dad never let us ride in those anyway. The track here wasn't good either, and a lot of times you had really rowdy people and undisciplined horses running. People did get hurt. The other two events, though, bothered me. Phil and I were entered in both, and this horse looked like he could win running backwards.

SCOUT

"Oh, well," I grinned weakly as I tried to dismiss the horse from my mind. "It'll be fun just to compete, I guess."

"Yeah," Randy responded. "Well, we'd better get back to the trailer before Scout has a fit."

"Um-hmm." We headed back the way we'd come. I'd told Scout to stay and watch the trailer, since Jennifer had gone with Phil to register. He would stay, I knew, but probably wouldn't like it.

We were threading our way through the ever-increasing crowd when we noticed that they were setting up part of the free-for-all course on the far end of the infield. We pushed our way up to the fence and took a quick look. They'd designed this event especially for today. I guess they were trying to present the competitors with the kind of riding they would do if they were going cross country, but the event was timed, just like all the others. You had to do everything right in order to qualify, but you still had to do it fast. We couldn't see much yet; so we turned to go.

For the second time in ten minutes, we discovered that there was someone standing right behind us, only this time we didn't recognize the guy. "Hi, boys," he said in a very friendly way. "Sorry, didn't mean to be in your way."

"S'okay," I said without thinking much about it. We were walking past him when he spoke again.

"Hey, aren't you from the family that found that Doberman?"

I turned back, surprised. "Yes, sir. Why?"

He shrugged and grinned. "Just curious. I've heard some about him. Haven't found any clues yet about where he came from, hmm?"

90

"No, sir."

"You must be having fun with him. I hear he's a pretty special dog."

"I like him." I wasn't sure I liked this man, but I couldn't have said why. I think maybe I just hated to have anyone ask questions about Scout for fear his real owner would turn up.

"What's he like?" The man persisted. "Really well trained? Good watchdog?"

"Boy, is he!" Randy apparently didn't share my inhibitions about talking to the stranger. "You wouldn't believe that dog. He patrols like he's one of the KGB on special assignment."

"You let him run around loose?" A frown crossed the man's face.

"Sure do," Randy continued enthusiastically. "The U.S. Marines couldn't sneak up on that house."

"Hmm." The man looked thoughtful. "Seems awfully funny that there's been no search for him by anybody. Wasn't he wearing a collar or anything when you found him?"

I shook my head. "Nothing but a choke collar, and it didn't have any tags."

"Don't forget the tube." Randy wanted to keep the floor.

"Tube?" The stranger's question was quick and interested. "What do you mean?"

"Oh, he found some piece of red foam rubber out in the channels, and he's in love with it." Randy, I knew, was winding up to go on all day. He loved to tell people things when they showed an obvious interest in what he was saying.

"Randy," I tried to cut him off, "forget it. It's time to go. I've got to get saddled up."

"Have you advertised the thing?" The man began to follow us as I half towed Randy away.

"Why?" Randy gave in and walked beside me. "It's nothing but a squishy chunk of foam. The dog's just weird, I think. Phil—this guy's brother—figures that somebody probably used to train him with something like that; so he's used to playing with it."

"Randy," I cut him off again, "would you be quiet!"

"Well, I was just—"

"I don't care! You don't have to tell the whole world!"

We were fixing to have a glaring argument when another friend of ours rode by on his horse, headed for the arena. "Hey, Jeff!" he called. "Some dog!"

"Yeah." I couldn't work up any great enthusiasm. I was beginning to wish I'd left Scout home.

The stranger stopped. "Do you have him with you?"

"Yeah," Randy started again. "Do you want to come and see him?"

"No," the man said abruptly. "I guess I'd better get going, too." He started away. "Nice talking to you guys."

We returned to the trailer in silence. I was angry at Randy, and I guess he wasn't very thrilled with me, either. Scout sat right where we'd left him, watching everyone and everything intently.

"Hi, dog." I greeted him with a pat. "You're popular, I guess."

"What's that?" Phil came around from the other side of the trailer.

"Scout's the number one topic of conversation today. Everybody's asking about him or talking about him."

Phil laughed. "Who?"

"Jerry, just a minute ago, and some guy I didn't know came up and started asking all kinds of questions about Scout and the tube."

"Really?" Phil frowned. "What kind of questions? And how did he know about the tube?"

"Blabbermouth told him." I indicated Randy with a jerk of my head as I picked up Cinder's saddle and went to my horse.

"Jeff!" Jennifer's soft rebuke didn't do much to improve my mood.

"Well, he doesn't have to go around telling the whole world everything all the time."

Phil's mind, however, was on the stranger. "I wish I knew who he was. If either of you sees him again, point him out to me. Seems funny that he was so curious when he doesn't even know us."

I ran the girth strap up tight and tucked the slack into the holder. Reaching for the bridle that hung on the horn, I made a try to change the subject. "Did you see Rod's new horse?"

"No, but I heard about him." Phil grinned. "Looks like we've got our work cut out for us today."

It didn't seem to bother him much. Phil loved challenges. I was feeling the adrenaline start to pump in me, too. This was the fun part, after all the work. When both horses were ready, we took them for a jog around the track to loosen them up. One more lap at an easy canter, then we returned to the trailer to fasten the elastic arm-band numbers close to our shoulders.

"What's the order of events?" I asked Phil.

"Barrels first, poles, keyhole, and pick-up. Then they're going to run the races and save the free-for-all for last."

"Well, good." I couldn't hide a smile. "Maybe Rod's horse will be tired out by the time we get to the free-for-all."

"Don't get your hopes up," Phil said dryly. "From what I hear, he may whip us all just by trotting around out there."

"Don't remind me. You haven't even seen him—I take that back. Look over there."

Phil twisted in his saddle to watch Rod riding by. I'm not sure if "ride" would be the most appropriate word. Cricket apparently knew what competition was all about—and also apparently tended to get a little excited about it. If I thought Cinder was bad, I was glad I wasn't riding that gray horse. He was progressing in leaps and twirls, tossing his head, rearing a little, and prancing all the time. Rod stuck to the saddle grimly, fighting to keep control of his mount.

Phil's shrill, long whistle split the air for a hundred yards in any direction. "Whoo-ee!" he exclaimed, drawing everyone's attention to the struggling rider. "Ride that horse, cowboy!"

"Soak your head, Wingate!" Rod yelled back, drawing laughter from the crowd.

Phil chuckled for a while. "Jeff, if he doesn't have any better control over him than that, I don't think we'll have anything to worry about in the free-for-all. And whoever he's riding partner with today will be lucky to get one shot at getting on him in the pick-up."

"Maybe." I still felt pretty intimidated by the long-legged gray. And it didn't improve my mood a little later to find out that his partner was none other than Mike Denal. "How in the world did that happen?" I glared at Phil when he reported the news.

"I guess he's just trying to be friendly to him, Jeff. Mike didn't have anybody else to pair up with. Maybe this way he'll learn to think a little better of the local people or at least won't hate living here so much if he finds something he likes to do."

"Hmmph," I grunted. "Two of the best horses in the state, and they've got to be riding together."

"We are here to compete." Phil didn't sound very pleased with me. "Rod's doing something to try to improve Mike's outlook—which is more than I've seen you do yet."

My face felt a little warm under his criticism, but I didn't have much time to think about it.

"Clear the track!" A scratchy voice boomed over the loudspeakers, making Cinder jump about two feet into the air. "Clear the track please! Barrel racing will begin in five minutes."

"Come on, Jeff," Phil wheeled Chance around. "They're playing our song!"

"Stay, Scout," I ordered the Doberman. "Watch the trailer, boy." Then I followed with Cinder, and we took our place among the milling bunch of horses and riders that were waiting for their number to be called. Jennifer and Randy would find a place in the stands, or more likely along the rail of the arena, if they could.

Cinder had already caught the excitement of the crowd. I was having a difficult time keeping him standing still when they started the runs around the barrels. Jerry Parks, the fellow I'd spoken to earlier, was the third rider to go, and he still held the top time when Phil's number was called. I knew I would be next; so I followed him to the starting area.

"Here goes nothing!" Phil grinned and rapped Chance with his heels. Watching Chance run through a course is like watching a professional exhibition. He never goofs. Phil charged him through the cloverleaf pattern and back across the finish line to the accompaniment of a lot of applause.

"Seventeen-two. Next!" the loudspeaker ordered. I swung Cinder into position at the very back of the starting area. He reared, knowing what was coming. I was expecting that though, and stood in my stirrups to force him down. He gave several little anxious jumps sideways, but I held him under a tight rein until he was facing the arena entry straight again.

"Easy, boy, easy, easy, now . . . ." I locked my hand around the saddle horn and half stood, leaning forward in the saddle. All at once, I let the reins loose and rapped out a sharp "Get up!"

He was off and running before you could blink. The challenge was always to slow him down enough to take the turns. I swung him to the barrel on the right, first, because that way he could make two turns on his favorite left lead. We made the first turn perfectly, tight and quick. A flying trip across the ring to the second barrel, a quick lead change, and we swung around again. A little far beyond the barrel, but he swung so sharp that my boot toe swung near the dusty ground.

Off to the third barrel at the far end of the arena. I tried to cut him in closer to the barrel this time, but I overdid it. My knee bumped into it, and I saw it rock crazily. I didn't look back to see whether or not it was going to fall. We made a mad charge back across the finish line, and only then did I realize that the crowd was cheering and whistling.

"Sixteen-two!" I heard from the loudspeaker. I grinned. I was up on Phil by a whole second. Cinder was snorting, not from shortness of breath, but from excitement. I knew now that he'd be nearly impossible to hold the next time out. Sometimes I wished they'd run the poles first, cause they're the hardest to control your horse in. And once Cinder got going—well, you know how it is.

Sure enough. I managed to stay in first place in the barrel running, and Phil held third. Rod and Cricket were disqualified for knocking over two of the three barrels; so we began to worry less about the speed-demon gray. He wasn't worth much if he couldn't be controlled. I was feeling pretty good then, but when it came to the poles, I was a total disaster. Cinder's time was close to five seconds away from placing. Chance ran the course like the pro he was, plunging through the poles like a skier on the slalom, changing leads every stride, rounding the top pole and sprinting back across the line to claim first place.

The keyhole was practically a re-run of the poles. I didn't feel as bad, though, because most of the riders had trouble getting their horses stopped within the limits of the tiny circle. Cinder overshot completely and disqualified himself. Phil took Chance the length of the arena at a dead run. At the opening of the key, he sat back in his saddle and lifted the reins. Chance all but sat down as he locked all four legs and slid into the circle. A rear, a spin, and a leap, and he was charging back to claim another first.

So far, things were going about as expected, but the pick-up was next. One thing about Indian pick-up— it's pretty hard to predict what is going to happen for anyone. Our turn came a whole lot sooner than I wanted it to. I was to be "picked up" on the first round; so I was waiting at the far end of the arena. When I saw Chance coming, I moved a step out beyond the barrel and back. I wanted to make sure he saw me. He had a habit of thinking Phil was cueing him for the barrel itself and just about mowing me over as he came around.

The big sorrel was really flying. This was competition, not practice, and he knew it. As he approached, I took two running steps to meet him and made a wild grab for the saddle horn. I felt its flat, hard edge catch the palm of my hand. I grabbed, pulled, and jumped. My right arm caught Phil around the waist and I was up. Holding my feet high to keep them clear of Chance's flying legs, I concentrated on keeping my balance until I saw the finish line flash beneath us.

Our time was read off, and we both heaved a sigh of relief. It wasn't outstanding, but it was good enough to keep us in the running. I figured we'd do better the second time. Phil is quicker than I am, and Cinder is quicker than Chance. By the time I was staring across the starting line to see Phil at the far end, Cinder was all tensed up again. I couldn't make him stand still to get a square start; so finally I just let him go. It was kind of rough going for the first few jumps, but by the time we went across the line into the arena, he had straightened out and was digging in so hard that dirt clods were sailing into the air twenty feet behind us.

Cinder knew what this was all about, and he headed straight for Phil. Twenty feet from the barrel I grabbed the reins in both hands and stood in the saddle. I leaned to the left and hauled back in a desperate effort to slow him and turn him at the same time. Well, we didn't slow much, but we did turn. Before I could guess how close we were to Phil, there was an arm in front of me, and I felt him on Cinder behind me. I pulled Cinder around to face the finish line and slammed my heels into his ribs. Phil and I were both screaming and yelling like Comanches all the way back across the ring. When Cinder shot across the line, there was no stopping him. He went clear across the prep area, onto the track, and off the other side, scattering competitors, spectators, and timers before him.

I wouldn't have been surprised if they'd disqualified us for disorderly conduct, but all we got was a bunch of dirty looks. We both got off Cinder, to make him settle down some, but it didn't work very well. Eventually, I took him back to the trailer to get him away from the excitement. I didn't want to stay, though; so I just tied him and started back to watch the last of the pick-up runs. Scout whined and begged to come, actually doing a little dance with his front feet.

"Okay." I gave in. "Come on. But you'd better behave." As it turned out, it was a good thing he did come.

Who else was starting their second run just as we rejoined Phil? None other but Rod and Mike. Mike was at the far end of the ring, waiting for Rod, who was having a terrible time getting Cricket back behind the timing line. A lot of the spectators were harassing and teasing him, and even from twenty feet away I could see that his face was a little red.

Even Phil was chuckling a little. "He's having a bad time now, Jeff, but they beat our best time by three seconds on their first round. That Mike is not a bad rider—not to mention that it looks like his horse knows all about contests."

To me, that sounded like a remark that was best left unanswered. I concentrated on Rod as he sent Cricket flying across the arena. Boy, that horse could run!

"Look out, look out!" I heard Phil muttering under his breath. Indeed, they were approaching the end of the arena without an iota of speed subtracted from the flying pace. Mike tried to get close to the tall gray anyway, and that's when it happened. Cricket shied away from him and went into a twisting, bucking fit. We couldn't really see what was happening, but we sure saw the gray horse fall. For a minute we thought he had gone down right on top of Mike, but he hadn't. The next second, Cricket was up and charging back for the break in the fence. Several of us tried to head him off, but we might as well have tried to stop a locomotive. He sent us scrambling left and right as he came through the gap about forty miles an hour.

It was shaping up to be great entertainment. Cricket tore off up the track, several riders urging their horses after him. They tried to spread out and box him in, but he was totally nuts. I heard people in the stands yelling at him as he broke through their line for the third time.

"They're never going to catch him that way." Phil was a little disgusted with the show.

I don't think of myself as brilliant, but every now and then I do get an idea. Right then, I looked at the short loop of the racing reins that hung loose from Cricket's bridle. They were close enough to the ground to be grabbed—a person probably wouldn't be quick enough, but the right dog might.

"Scout!" My voice was low, but his ears pricked up. I snapped my fingers and swept my hand in a line to draw his attention to the horse that was fleeing down the track again. "Catch him. Bring him here. Go!"

I hadn't been sure that he would understand, but he was off and running before I had fairly completed the order. A surprised murmur went through the crowd as the Doberman sailed over the low track fence and cut in at an angle toward Cricket. It wasn't much to watch, really. Scout was at the gray's head before the horse knew what was happening. A single jump, and he had the reins in his mouth. Cricket must have been tiring out or something, because he yielded to the drag on his bridle almost immediately and slowed to a halt. If he had fought hard, the bridle probably would have broken. As it was, one of the guys who had been chasing just stopped his horse, got off, walked up, and took the bridle from Scout.

As he did so, I stuck a couple fingers in my mouth and whistled. Scout came back at the same flying pace that he'd left, panting and wriggling in excitement from all the praise I gave him. The crowd went wild, too, applauding, whistling, and cheering.

"Come on," Phil urged me. "Let's get back to the trailer. I'm starved. It's a good thing you got your share of the glory here, because their time sure beat ours—look."

Sure enough. The posted winners had us in second place, losing to Mike and Rod's first run. I didn't feel real great about that but managed to pull myself together enough to congratulate Mike when we crossed his path on the way back.

"Thanks," he muttered, abruptly turning the other direction, Casper in tow.

"Of all the—" I started sputtering.

"Stop it, Jeff." Phil's voice was patient and quiet. "It's going to take a while. Just keep your end up, okay?"

Chapter Ten
A Major Breakthrough

The free-for-all wouldn't be until after lunch; so we had to put the horses up for a while and go get something to eat. By the time we had the horses cooled out and taken care of, Jennifer and Randy had arrived. The picnic lunch was soon being devoured. Scout sat by the edge of the blanket, too well trained to actually beg, but his eyes pleaded every time I took a bite. I managed to slip him a few pieces when no one was looking. That wasn't too hard, because conversation was all about Chance and Cinder, and no one was paying much attention to Scout.

He changed that though, all of a sudden. He interrupted one of Randy's long observations with a low growl. We all stared at him in surprise. He was looking away from us, toward the track.

"What's the matter with you?" Phil asked him, sort of in a joking tone.

Scout answered by sharpening the growl into a full-fledged, lip-curled snarl. His head went down, and he stood up, tentatively sniffing the air. I felt a tingling chill go down my spine. I'd never seen him do that before. All the hair on his back was standing straight up.

"Scout!" I spoke sharply. "Quiet. Down, now. What's all this fuss about?" I glanced at the milling crowd that was all around.

"He must see someone or something he doesn't like," Jennifer commented as Scout sat down unwillingly and quit growling.

"What, though?"

"I don't know, but he doesn't act like that for no reason."

Scout was quiet, but he continued to face the track. Stiff and alert he sat, and he didn't so much as look at me again. I thought he was mad at me for scolding him, and I tried to make up by offering him a left-over tuna sandwich when lunch was over, but he just sniffed it and turned his attention back toward the crowd. His ears dropped from their alert pose for just a moment, and he stuck his head under my hand to be petted, but soon he was engaged in his own personal staredown again.

We were cleaning up when Jerry dropped by. "Hi, you guys. Pretty good show you're making today."

"Us or the dog?" Phil said dryly.

"Both." He laughed. "Hey, d'ya hear what happened to Rod?"

"No, what?" Phil snapped the locks down on the top of the cooler.

"Broke his arm in two places and snapped three or four ribs. He wasn't feeling too good I guess."

"I guess not."

They continued talking, but for some reason, I started thinking of Mike. That meant he no longer had a partner for the free-for-all. In a way I was almost glad, but a niggling little feeling wouldn't leave me alone. I kept thinking about Phil's remark earlier that day—that I hadn't done much to be friendly. When Jerry finally left, I waited until I could talk to Phil alone.

"Do you think Mike will find anybody else to ride with?"

Phil stopped, turned, and stared at me. "I doubt it." His reply was thoughtful, and he turned back to folding up the blanket.

"Think they would let me ride twice?" I didn't look up at him. I wasn't sure how he was going to take this.

"I doubt that, too."

I could tell by his voice that he was smiling; so I looked up.

"They might let you change your registration, though, if you'd ride with him instead of with me." Phil's voice was so nonchalant that I couldn't tell if he was for or against the idea.

I didn't answer right away. I knew Phil liked to compete, but I knew, too, that he had wanted me to do something to try to make up for what had happened last week. "Would you mind?" I finally blurted out. "You wouldn't be able to ride, then."

"Of course not, Jeff." He almost started laughing. "If I'd have thought I could make you do it, I would have anyway. It's far more important that you make an effort to be friends with Mike."

I could feel my face flush again; so I turned away quickly. "I'll go ask him."

"I'll go have the pairings changed." Phil started off in the other direction.

"Not yet! He might not want to."

"I have to do it now or it'll be too late—so you'd better be convincing."

Sighing, I started off in the direction I'd seen Mike heading with Casper. Scout stalked beside me, alert and stiff, glaring around like he was expecting every person in the crowd to jump on me and beat me up.

"What is the matter with you, dog?" I couldn't get over his strange behavior, but there was no way to find out why he was acting that way. It didn't take long to find the Denals. Casper is a pretty easy horse to pick out of a crowd. Mike was starting to load him onto a trailer when I walked up.

"Hi." I knew it was dumb to say that and nothing else, but I was a little short on brainstorms for speeches just then.

"Wha'cha want?" Mike was his usual, tactful self. I saw no point in wasting time.

"I want you to ride in the free-for-all with me."

He stopped halfway up the trailer ramp and looked over Casper's back at me. "You're nuts."

"No, I'm not. Your partner's cracked up; so you don't have anybody to ride with. Except for Cricket, we've probably got the fastest horses here—and he won't be in it; so we can mop up."

I saw a glint appear in his eye, but he still turned away. "Nah, I don't think so."

A familiar irritation surged up in me. I tried to squash it down before it took over, but I didn't quite make it. "What's the matter? You chicken?"

For a second, I thought he was going to jump off the back of the trailer at me. I took a hasty step back. "Come on, Mike, I'm just kidding. Why won't you? We can beat 'em all—and Phil's already gone to change the entry pairings."

He was quiet for a moment. I thought he was going to say no again, but finally he reversed Casper's direction, backing him off the ramp.

"All right." His voice was kind of quiet. "I guess we can try."

"Try what?" Mr. Denal came around the side of the trailer, only catching the last sentence.

I didn't answer but just dropped my hand on Scout's head and looked at Mike. He led Casper to his saddle. "I guess we're going to try the free-for-all."

"Who is?" Mr. Denal was a little slow to catch on.

"We are," Mike said brusquely.

"We? Oh!" Mr. Denal looked at me, breaking out in a smile like I'd just handed him a thousand dollars. "Well, what do you know! I, uh, well," his voice trailed away when neither of us said anything more. "Well, I guess your mother and I will go back over and get a seat so we can watch. Ah, good luck." He backed around the corner of the trailer and disappeared.

I glanced at Mike and said, "I'll go get Cinder and be right back.

Mike grunted something that might have been "Yeah."

There wasn't time for us to practice together, not even once; so it's a good thing that we both knew what to do. We sat outside the bigger of the two arenas, watching the horses before us do their rounds. The free-for-all was going to be tricky. For most of it, you just had to ride around and through a bunch of obstacles. The hitch there was the fifteen-foot piece of string that has to be tied from the saddle horn of your saddle to the one on your partner's saddle. You weren't supposed to go far enough apart to break it. If you did, they'd dock your time by fifteen seconds, which is usually enough to throw you out of placing. So if you can't control your horse very well, this isn't the contest for you.

When you finish the obstacle course, you have to switch horses, do a lap around the outside of the course, which includes two low jumps, and switch again without dismounting. Then, one of you has to go to the far end of the ring, get a wooden baton from one of the judges, and bring it back to the other, who takes it back to the judge. Your time is up when the second person crosses the line on the way back.

We were the last to go; so we knew what time we had to beat: 6:37:09. I must admit that I wasn't very confident as we started out. We had a rough time of it with the obstacle course. Cinder wouldn't hang as close to Casper as he would to Chance, and he fought me most of the way through. We cantered where we could and trotted when we couldn't: through the maze, over the wooden bridge, under the rope, through the cones, around the barrel, through the ditch, over the low jump (we almost lost it, there), and finally up to the gate. When we got on the other side we could break the string and forget it. The plan had been for me to open the gate and Mike to close it, but when we got close, Cinder decided he didn't like the looks of it.

"Hurry up!" Mike's voice was low but lacked nothing in intensity. "Move him."

"He won't move!" I slammed my heels against his ribs but only succeeded in making him leap to the side. The string stretched to its capacity. Mike, his face calm and composed, sent Casper right behind us, putting himself alongside the gate. Quickly, and neater than he could have done it from the ground, he leaned over, popped the latch, and swung it open. He tensed Casper's reins and the flashy Appaloosa backed through, one quick step after another, while I beat a tattoo on Cinder's ribs to make him follow frontwards. Before he could start giving me trouble again and move me out of range, I gave the gate a hard back-kick, slamming it securely shut. The bang sent both horses leaping in opposite directions. They broke the string, but it didn't matter now.

Jumping off, we threw reins at each other and scrambled for the saddles again. Casper was a lot shorter than Cinder, and all my recent work for Indian pick-up paid off. I landed squarely in his saddle without touching a stirrup. Somehow or other, Mike pulled himself aboard the dancing Cinder. "You first!" I yelled at him.

Really, I could have saved my breath. He didn't have a choice. Cinder was off like a shot. Mike's only hope was to guide him in the right direction. Casper charged along behind him. I didn't even have to urge him. He seemed to know what this was all about. He was easier to guide than Cinder—responsive to the slightest shift of the reins. But I had trouble adjusting to his stride. After Cinder's long-legged, ground-gulping flow, Casper's seemed choppy and rough.

Both horses flew over the low jumps like they weren't even there, but I could see Mike having trouble pulling Cinder down as we reached the area where we had to switch back. "Drag on him!" I yelled again. "Hard!"

111

"Just get over here!" Mike yelled back. I could see his jaw clenched in determination as he fought to force Cinder close enough to reach out and grab Casper's bridle. The Appaloosa was amazingly cooperative. It was almost like riding Chance. I dug my heel into his side and he responded with a quick, neat sidestep that brought him right up beside Cinder. Mike grabbed his bridle and I abandoned ship. Hitching a knee up on the saddle to brace myself, I leaned over, grabbed the back of Cinder's saddle, and very ungraciously dragged myself over.

Even though he was used to it, Cinder never liked this. He jumped a little and started to prance again. Mike almost stretched himself in two trying to keep him under control and keep a hold on Casper at the same time. "Come on!" I was amazed that he wasn't yelling at me. Mike's voice was cool as a cucumber. "Hurry up—get his reins."

Frantically, I reached around him and grabbed Cinder's reins. The second I had them, Mike was out from in front of me, belly-flopped across Casper's saddle. With a quick, very coordinated jerk, he pulled himself astride the saddle and sent Casper tearing toward the far end of the ring. I was having problems of my own trying to scramble over the back of the saddle in time to keep Cinder from following. We were barely in position when Mike and Casper came flying toward us.

"Now!" Once again, Mike's voice was sharp, but very, very calm. I extended my hand as far out from Cinder as I could. Mike slammed the baton squarely into my palm. I took a death grip on it and let Cinder go. We were at the end of the ring in less time than it takes to say it. I didn't even bother trying to stop Cinder.

I just wheeled him around the judge like I would have a barrel, dropping the baton into his hands as we went, then sent Cinder flying for the finish line.

Every split second counted, and I whacked the big bay a couple times with the ends of the reins. He went across the line like the twelve o'clock express, once again overshooting by a good hundred feet before I could stop him. I was winded worse than he was. I gasped and leaned over in my saddle, not paying much attention to the clamor going on around me, until someone roughly dragged me out of my saddle.

"Hey!" I exclaimed, "What are you—"

"Six thirty-five!" Mike was bellowing in my ear. He let go of me, and I almost fell on my face. "Wake up, man! We did it! We won!"

I spit some dust out of my mouth. "We did?" I looked at him in amazement, realizing that I'd never seen him smile before. He was grinning so high that it almost touched his ears. "Well, what d'ya know." I really was surprised. Then I started to feel good. Awfully good.

To my further surprise, Mike was holding out his hand. I took it tentatively and responded to his handshake. "Not bad for a backwoods native," he said with a grin.

I had to smile, too. "Not too bad for a stuck-up city slicker, either," I retorted.

He took a mock swing at me. "Go catch your horse, native. I'll see you later."

Cinder really was getting some ideas about taking off; so I had to turn my attention to him. What was left of the afternoon was interesting, though. Mr. Denal came to our trailer and showered both Phil and me with a million thank-yous. "You have no idea how much this has done for Mike," I heard him telling Phil after I had moved away.

"It's been good for Jeff, too." Phil's voice was steady. "I hope he and Mike can get to know each other better. We'd like to see more of you and your family."

"He's been so sure that he was going to hate it here— this is the first move anyone his age has really made to try to be friendly with him." Mr. Denal rattled on enthusiastically.

I quit listening, feeling a little guilty. It hadn't been so hard to do, I guess. So why hadn't I tried a little harder before? Oh well. At least I could try to make up for some lost time.

Before long, we were rolling out of the fairgrounds. We honked and waved at Denals' suburban and trailer as they passed us. Randy and I were standing up in the back of our pickup, leaning over the top of the cab. "See ya!" I yelled. "Come on out for a ride Monday morning!"

Mike yelled something back that I couldn't quite hear, but it sounded like some kind of an agreement.

A stiff breeze had sprung up, swirling up the dust that had been pounded around all day. It got into our eyes, making us blink and squint. Only Scout stood, leaning over the side of the truck bed, nose into the wind, testing and searching like he'd been doing all day. I shook my head in puzzlement and turned my back to the wind. We were just pulling out of the gate as I turned, and suddenly I saw the fellow that had stopped Randy and me earlier.

"Hey, Phil!" I pounded on the roof of the cab. He rolled his window down, and I leaned around a little bit. "There's that guy we were telling you about—the nosy one. Over there in the blue Chevette. See?"

Phil slowed down even more, craning his neck to get a good look at the stranger. "Don't think I know him either, Jeff." We all inspected the man closely for another moment. Suddenly, he turned his head and noticed all of us staring at him. Abruptly, he cut off the conversation he'd been carrying on with another man, rolled up the window, and drove away.

Shaking his head, Phil let the truck start rolling ahead again. He said something to Jennifer, but I couldn't hear what it was. When we pulled out on the road and picked up speed, Randy and I both stretched out on the floor of the cab to get out of the wind. Scout came around and lay down beside me, stretching his head across my stomach. I lay there, watching the bright blue sky and patches of clouds stream by above me, and drifted to sleep to the vibrating of the motor beneath me.

Chapter Eleven
A Close Call

Once the barrier had gone down between Mike and me, we found it easier to put up with each other. Before I really realized what was happening, we had begun spending more and more time together. Phil and Jennifer spent a lot of time with Mr. and Mrs. Denal, and I knew that Randy's parents were seeing quite a bit of them, too. So it wasn't very surprising, even, that they visited church with us a couple times. Both our family and the Kellers were praying that all of the Denals would be saved soon.

Meanwhile, Randy and I were having fun. We hadn't had anyone new to hang around with for a long time. Mike, once he decided to let himself like his new home a little, kept us entertained with stories from the West and California, where neither Randy or I had ever been. Mike and I were thinking about teaming up the next summer to do some more competing. I was pretty sure Dad would let me, and Mr. Denal was all for it. Personally, I loved the idea, and it was good to have someone my own age around who thought like I did about the contests. I mean, Randy likes to ride and everything, but he doesn't really take it very seriously—seriously enough to work at it and be good enough to compete. Maybe if he had his own horse it would be different.

For our part, though, Randy and I spent a lot of time trying to change Mike's outlook on living in the Les Cheneaux Islands. We went out in the *Luau,* took him fishing (there's nothing like a fresh perch dinner to put a fellow in a good frame of mind), talked a lot about the not-too-distant opening of school, and even coaxed Randy's Dad into taking us on a drive through what we call "the hardwoods" one day. All of Les Cheneaux is beautiful, but there are a lot of different kinds of scenery. When you get north of the water a few miles, the land gets higher and the forests change almost completely. Instead of pine, cedar, and brush, you have tall maple, beech, birch, oak—and almost no undergrowth. All kinds of little gravel roads twist and turn through those big woods. In the summer, they're little more than tunnels underneath the arches of the trees that meet overhead.

It's a really neat place to explore; so while Mr. Keller sat in the car listening to the broadcast of the Tigers' baseball game, we took a hike up to Dagget Tower, which is the highest spot on the eastern end of the peninsula between Lake Huron and Lake Superior. Standing up there beside it, you can look down the open spaces that have been cut through the woods for the power lines. To the north, you can't see much but woods. To the south the land drops sharply, and you can see out over the farmland below you, all the way to the water and beyond. Even the five-mile-long Mackinac Bridge looks like a toy, sitting there on the skyline. That bridge is the only route to the lower peninsula of Michigan.

"Have you ever been across it?" Randy asked Mike as we sat on the steep slope and looked out.

"No. We drove in from Wisconsin."

"We'll have to go over and walk it on Labor Day," I said. "That way you can get a really good look."

"Why Labor Day?" Mike frowned.

"'Cause that's the only day they let people walk across," Randy explained with flawless logic. "Other than that it's vehicles only."

"It's a long walk, but fun." I thought of the thousands of people that hiked across the huge suspension bridge every September. "Usually the governor, or somebody else important, leads off. Sometimes they'll have races and stuff like that, but just to go up there is worth it. When you get to the middle section, around where the towers are, half of the road under your feet is nothing but a steel grill, like covers over the holes in sidewalks."

"Why?" Mike didn't sound like he liked that idea very much.

"Because it's a suspension bridge. It hangs from those two towers. If the wind got blowing hard enough, it would cause too much movement of the bridge. With the grills there, it blows through instead of against. See?"

"Yeah, I guess." Mike's eyes were glued on the distant structure.

"Well," Randy cut in on my course of bridge history, "we'd better scram back down. Dad said he had to be home by five. And he's going to be tired of waiting on us anyway."

We retraced our steps back past the big red and white police tower and took a shortcut down the open power trail on the opposite side of the hill. "Mom loves it up here in the spring," Randy panted as we trotted along.

"Why's that?" Mike was repeating that phrase a lot today.

"Wild lilies!"

"Wild lilies?" There was disbelief in Mike's voice.

"Trilliums, really, I guess is what they're called." Randy was apparently unwilling to be left out of Mike's education about his new home area. "Wildflowers grow up here in the spring, in a way that puts professional greenhouses to shame! You can't put your foot down between 'em: adder's-tongues, Dutchman's-breeches, violets, mayflowers, jack-in-the-pulpits, lady's-slippers, lilies . . . "

"He'll see them himself someday." When we reached the level field, I interrupted Randy's discourse. "Come on—I'll race you to the car!"

It wasn't too many mornings later that I woke up to the realization that the summer was almost over. A check with the wall calendar confirmed it—August 10. With a shock I realized that Mom and Dad would be home in ten days. "Jennifer! Hey Jennifer!" I started downstairs on the run.

"What in the world is worth this kind of commotion at six-thirty in the morning?" Her soft voice warned me that Phil was probably still asleep.

"Mom and Dad are going to be home in ten days!"

"Yes, I know." She smiled. "When did this dawn on you?"

Her faint sarcasm was lost on me. I had something else on my mind. "Hey, Jen, if I can get some blueberries, will you make some homemade blueberry ice cream? We could put it in the freezer and keep it until they get here. Mom likes that better than anything—it would be a good welcome-home treat and—"

I guess she could see that I was prepared to talk her to death until she agreed, because she stopped me. "Whoa, boy! Whoa. Okay. On one condition: that you get enough to make a pie for us before they get home. If you bring fresh blueberries into this house and I don't make a pie, your brother will throw me out."

"Deal," I said.

"Really, Jeff, don't you think it's a little early for the berries to be ripe?"

"Well, it's been really warm. Anyway, it'll be fun to go up and hunt around. I'm going to call Randy and Mike and see if they want to ride up to Bay City Lake."

"Ride? Are you crazy? I'll drive you up. You'll be all day getting up there and back. At least that way, if you don't find anything, you won't have wasted so much time."

"No, come on! Let us ride. We haven't gone out on a long ride in ages."

"Well, all right. If Phil okays it."

"He will." He did, too. It turned out that Mike was going to go, but Randy couldn't. His mother was taking him shopping for school clothes. He wasn't very excited about the idea, but she wasn't giving him a choice.

Mike and I were on our way by eight o'clock. The route we had to take to get to Bay City Lake was quite a trip, counting a stretch where we had to follow Highway 134 for a way. The horses were used to the traffic, though; so it was really no big deal. Scout trailed along with us like a veteran trailblazer. Tied to the saddle, we carried lunch, containers for berries, and tethers for the horses.

Bay City Lake is really sort of a campground/picnic place. Not the greatest for swimming, if that's what you have in mind, but it's one of the few places right around our area that're any good for blueberries. Most places are too swampy, or else too overgrown with spruce and pine trees. It's a really pretty ride up there. Once we crossed over to the north side of 134, we took to the woods. There's a maze of trails between the highway and the dirt roads that run around the lake and the campground. Most of them are trails that are used by the snowmobile clubs in the winter; so the ground on some of them is really rocky and rough. If you know where you're going, though, you can make a really nice ride of it.

You could tell that summer was getting late just by looking around and breathing. The underbrush was grown up high and fully leafed out. Ragweed and wild mustard grew in the open spots, high enough to nearly reach our shoulders if we had been walking. In the spring and early summer, the woods are kind of bare and usually smell damp. Now, every breath you took hinted at herbs and sage. We spotted several deer drifting lazily through the forest—another proof of the season. They were fat and lazy. In the spring, they're as nervous and jumpy as Repeat is all the time.

As we drew closer to the lake area, the trails broadened out, grew drier and more sandy. The trees were different, too. Not so much spruce. More hardwood, and all of them a lot more sparse than back in the thick of the woods.

By the time we got to the lake itself, we were ready for a drink, and the horses were too. We spent a while cooling off and lightening our load by a couple of Cokes before moving on down toward the west end of the lake. I knew from experience that if there were any berries, they'd be down there. Sure enough. It didn't take much hunting at all before we found a likely looking spot. We loosened the girths on Cinder and Casper, took their bridles off, and put on the halters and tethers that we'd brought. We knew it would take a while to fill the containers we'd brought, and you just don't leave horses standing around tied by their bridles—especially not horses like Cinder. At least not if you care what happens to your bridle.

By lunch time, we had most of the containers filled; so we stopped and ate. We had a few berries to go with the sandwiches, too.

"You know," I commented as we picked up the last of the containers, "I didn't think the picking would be so good, really. We should have had Phil drive up to take the berries back, at least. They're probably going to be squashed by the time they make it back in those guys' saddlebags."

"Nah!" Mike snickered. "Tupperware is tough! We'll just have to make sure that none of the seals come undone, or we will have a mess—horse sweat-blueberry stew."

"Gross."

"Just think what fun Jennifer would have with that—umm! What an addition to blueberry ice cream."

I pretended to take a swing at him. He threw a handful of blueberries at me and ran. Of course, without thinking, I ran right after him. So I guess, in a way, what happened was really my fault. I should have told him in the first place, and I should have known better than to do it anyway, but there are some things that you just don't do in blueberry spots around Bay City Lake in mid-August. Charging through without paying attention to what's around you is high on the list.

In no time at all, Mike was running as fast as he could through the high undergrowth. Suddenly he took an abrupt turn and crashed through between a couple of high bushes, then tripped and fell—almost on top of a gamboling, first-year, black bear cub. I heard its squealing grunt before I saw it, and my heart shot right up into my throat.

"Mike! Get out of there! Get up—come on—run!" I don't know if he heard me or not. I guess the cub had scared the wits out of him before he realized what it was. Once he realized, he was just mad, and he didn't think about the fact that mama would be nearby.

"Hey, you little slob—beat it!" He threw two of the containers at it. One struck the little thing, and it started squealing again. Suddenly there was another little, black fuzz-ball bounding by. Together, the two of them scrambled up a nearby tree, squealing indignantly.

Then I heard what I'd dreaded: a coughing growl from the thicket to the other side. I panicked. We were in the worst possible spot—right beside the she-bear's crying babies and between her and them. She didn't know what was happening to them, but she was coming to fix it. "Mike! We're gonna get killed—run! Run!"

My yelling and hollering finally got through to him; plus he heard the popping and crashing as the mother sprinted toward us. A bulky-looking bear can cover an astonishing amount of ground in a very short time period. I'd always been taught to climb a skinny tree if I ever got in trouble with a bear, but in that moment, reason deserted me.

Mike and I fled through the underbrush, back the way we'd come. As long as it seemed, I guess it wasn't but twenty seconds since Mike had first fallen. It wouldn't have been another ten before that bear was on top of us, but, from out of nowhere, all of a sudden Scout was between me and her. He was as mad as she was. He stood his ground, thundering a series of challenging barks, daring her to continue her charge. She dared. The big dog and the huge bear tangled in a rolling, thrashing twist of black bodies. The roaring, snarling, and yelling barks blended together in one almost continuous sound.

By all rights, Scout should have died in the first rush he made, and I'll never know why he didn't. I do know that he gave me a chance, and I took it. Panic put wings on my feet—Mike's too. Barely conscious of the raging, cutthroat struggle going on behind us, we flew back to the horses as fast as we could go.

Both of them were fighting their tethers in total panic. They had caught the bear-smell. Just before I reached him, Cinder gave a final plunge, breaking his tie with a resounding pop. He took off in a mad charge down the trail. Casper threw a real fit then. We reached him barely in time. I grabbed his halter while Mike vaulted up on his back. I jerked the tether loose and threw him the loose end.

"Come on!" he yelled at the same moment, holding his hand down to me. With a means of escape right in front of me, I suddenly realized that my dog was probably being torn apart by a 400-pound hulk of fury.

"Go get help!" I yelled at Mike, turning away.

"You're crazy—come on!" He grabbed at my shoulder, but at that moment, a crazy tangle of furious dog and murderous bear tumbled out of the brush two hundred feet from us, sounding like war animals from African jungles. Mike no longer had a choice. With just the halter, Casper took advantage of his rider and tore off after Cinder, back toward the campground.

I stood transfixed. At that distance, I couldn't tell what was dog and what was bear. I could taste the fear in my mouth. No dog fights with a bear and survives— but there was nothing, absolutely nothing, I could do to help. I wondered if I was imagining what I was seeing until they moved more out into the open and I could see that Scout wasn't so much fighting with her as taunting her. It was a hair-splitting game of life and death that the Doberman was playing, darting back and forth, whirling, nipping, dodging, leaping. A single solid blow from one of those huge paws would have killed him more surely than a bullet into his heart.

I wasn't really conscious of praying, but suddenly, an answer to prayer came around the curve of the two-track dirt road. A jeep careened over the rough bumps, several young men in it shouting at the tops of their voices. It spun to a halt and I saw the guy in the passenger seat stand up and level a shotgun at the bear.

"Don't!" I screamed. "You'll hit my dog!"

But I was too late. The gun exploded. To my surprise, the bear whipped around to face the jeep, another roar tearing out of her. Scout was on her in a second, from the back. She whirled on him again, and the fellow in the truck emptied the other barrel. When she swung to face them again, I was ready. My shrill two-fingered whistle split the air from there to the far end of the lake.

Scout reacted instantly, bounding toward me. Never before had I been so glad that someone had trained him to obey in a split second. I saw the guy in the truck break the stock of the gun with lightning speed, eject, and insert more shells. As the she-bear stood, snarling her indecision, he pumped another load into her. I figured it couldn't have been any more than birdshot in the gun because it didn't seem to be doing much harm. The bear gave a last coughing roar and lumbered into the woods.

I saw no more. My arms were full of a frantic, whining, panting, bleeding Scout. Tears mingled with the blood that ran down my arms as I tried to staunch the flow from the horrible gash along his rib cage. Several smaller cuts decorated his shoulders and head, but the side cut was pouring blood so fast that it was actually dripping onto the sandy soil at my feet. He tried to lick my face but coughed and gagged a little. I didn't know if he was just sick from exhaustion or if he had internal injuries as well.

The jeep pulled up beside me. Four roughly-dressed men in their early twenties dropped out of it beside me. "Hey, kid—you all right?" one of them asked me. "We heard a bear—we know the sound, believe me—then all the other ruckus, and somebody yelling; so we made tracks."

"I'm all right." I gritted my teeth and tried to stop crying. "But my dog—"

"Yeah, I see your dog." Another of the men was kneeling beside Scout, on the other side. "He's got to get to a vet, quick. Where are your folks?"

"Not here. I mean, I live here—I mean we were on horses and they took off."

"Who?"

"A friend—he went to the campground to get help."

"Where d'ya live?" The first one spoke again.

"Down on the lake—my Dad's Alan Wingate."

"You're Wingate's kid? Phil's brother?"

"Yeah—"

"Come on." the men stood up all together. "We're taking you and this guy to the vet. We'll call your brother from there. There's no time to wait for him to get up here."

Before I could think of any reason why I should protest, we were in the jeep, tearing down the rough trail as fast as they dared. We hadn't gone a hundred yards though, when we met Mike coming toward us, riding like the warring Sioux were on his trail. Behind him came a bouncing, swaying pickup. Everyone stopping at once kicked up so much dust we could hardly see each other.

"We're okay!" I yelled at him. "But we're taking Scout to the vet. He's cut. Can you find Cinder?"

"Yeah—but is it safe to stay around here?"

"Buddy," the jeep driver spat over the side, "stay on that horse, and you'll be fine. You couldn't force him within half a mile of that bear."

"Okay." Mike pulled Casper off the trail. "I'll get him and go home, but you'd better call Phil before I get there."

"I will!" I had to yell over my shoulder because the jeep was taking off again. The driver of the pickup that had been following Mike had apparently sized up the situation correctly, because he backed off the narrow road to let us go by.

All in all, that was the bumpiest ride I've ever taken. These guys had no respect for holes or roots in the road. We flew out of there like we were on a paved highway. By the time we did reach the main road, Scout had quieted in my arms. He lay there, still panting a little bit, but otherwise motionless. His eyes looked a little glassy.

I crooned to him and praised him in a way that I'm sure General Patton never was praised in his lifetime. I barely heard the driver introducing himself and his companions. His name—Greg Brailer—was the only one I recognized. I wouldn't have recognized him though, I don't think. Well, maybe. I guess I'd seen him around town. Anyway, he started telling me that he and Phil had graduated from high school together.

"I guess I could have guessed that you're a Wingate," he remarked as we made the last turn toward the vet's clinic. "You're the spittin' image of your brothers."

"Don't worry about your mutt," one of the others said. "He looks a little chewed up, but I don't think any of them are more than surface wounds—and we're out here quick enough to keep him from bleeding to death."

The little jeep rocked into the driveway and screeched to a halt. Greg jumped out, came around, and picked up Scout like he would have a little puppy. "Get up there and get the door open," he ordered.

Chapter Twelve

The Summer's Almost Over

Dr. Anderson wasn't sure he was happy to see me. He rolled his eyes and looked exasperated, but as soon as Greg brought Scout through the door, he sprang into action. We were all barred from the dispensary; so I went to the receptionist's desk to make a phone call. I wasn't looking forward to it, but it had to be done.

"Hi, Jennifer?" I winced visibly.

"Jeff! Where in the world are you calling from?"

"Ah, um, is Phil there?"

"Well, yes, but—"

"Could I talk to him, please?"

Phil's voice came on the line quickly. "What's up, Jeff? Where are you?" I took a deep breath and closed my eyes.

"Um, we're at the vet's."

"Great. What happened? Porcupine?"

"No." I swallowed. "Actually—it was—listen, Phil, everybody's fine, but um—actually it was a bear."

"A what? Wait a minute, how did you get up there, anyway—and how in the world—" I snatched the phone away from my ear. The volume of his voice could be heard across the room. Greg walked over to me, grinning. He took the phone, and I didn't fight him.

"Hey, Wingate!" He chuckled into the receiver. "Cool off. The kid's fine." The noise from the other end of the line quieted.

"This's Greg Brailer—well, I'm not rightly sure. We haven't discussed this in detail yet. Just got here. But I guess the kids came on the bear at the lake and the dog tore into it to keep it off of 'em—nah! He's a little cut up, but he'll be all right. I'll tell ya'—I never did see the likes of that dog. (Pause) No, Carl pumped her full of birdshot. Was all we had in the jeep, but it did the trick. (Longer pause) I guess he went after your brother's horse. He ought to be along—maybe. Wouldn't hurt, I guess. Yeah, okay. We'll bring him home."

Greg hung up and grinned at me again. "Don't sweat it, Jeff. He'll settle down. Wasn't like you did it on purpose or something."

"That's for sure." I sat down, suddenly feeling awfully tired. I couldn't make myself read a magazine or anything, but even so, the wait seemed awfully short. Dr. Anderson was back out with us, being his usual cheerful self.

"I don't know what you people think a dog's for— always bringing him out here cut to pieces. . . ." He mumbled on while I signed a charge slip.

Scout, to my surprise, was fit enough to walk out by himself. Dr. Anderson gave me a tin of ointment to keep the cuts from drying out and a bottle of antibiotic capsules to ward off infection. Other than that, the cut on his side was the only place that even had any stitches.

"The other places don't really need it," Dr. Anderson told us. "And he'd just be chewing at them anyway."

He stepped back and surveyed Scout critically. "At least he'll match." The vet pointed to the old scar running down Scout's other side. "But you'll know what made this one."

By the time the jeep bounced into our yard, Mike had returned with the horses. He'd caught up with Cinder halfway home and brought him back. Phil had helped him cool the horses off and call his parents. Now everybody was waiting there, on the back deck, for us, listening to Mike recount the story for about the fifth time.

I could tell right away that Jennifer had been crying. She jumped up, came to me, and hugged me the minute I stepped out of the jeep. Scout jumped stiffly to the ground and stood beside me a little unsteadily. Suddenly I was forgotten in the general hubbub of people that crowded around him, all wanting to pet him and praise him at the same time.

He took a step back and twitched his tail in surprise. He had plenty of time to get used to it, though, because everyone stayed for supper, and Scout was the hero of the evening. He got the whole microwaved beefsteak while the rest of us ate charcoal-grilled hamburgers.

I was dog-tired that night, if you'll pardon the expression, and went to bed as soon as everyone had left. Phil didn't even chew me out for being careless. I guess that was tribute to the fact that he was glad I was alive. So was I.

The rest of the week was filled with preparations for Mom and Dad's homecoming. Jennifer drafted both Phil and me into her cleaning service, and we scrubbed and dusted from attic to basement. After that, the boats had to be done, then the barn. Lawn to trim, beach to rake, porch to paint—there wasn't much time for riding. Which was just as well, I guess, because Scout would have wanted to go along and he was still pretty stiff.

Over the weekend, though, he seemed to perk up and get over the worst of it. It got so that you could only see the limp when he was running. He was getting almost spoiled from being the center of everyone's attention. We took him back to the vet's the first of the week to have his stitches taken out. Dr. Anderson pronounced him healthy, if a little scarred.

Early in that week, some of Phil and Jennifer's friends came to visit. They were another couple, Chris and Lisa, who taught in their school. They'd never been in northern Michigan before; so we spent a lot of time showing them around. We went up to Sault Ste. Marie and took them on a tour of the locks: the huge raising and lowering devices that allow the big freighters to get on and off Lake Superior from the St. Marys River, which is much lower. They're one of the biggest systems in the world, sitting right on the border between us and Canada.

We took them over to Mackinac Island, which is one of Michigan's famous places. Really, I'm not too wild about it—it's pretty much just a big tourist trap. There are no cars over there. Just horses and bicycles. They sell tons of fudge on the island and every other kind of trinket souvenir you can imagine. We had lunch at the Grand Hotel and took everybody's pictures out on its front porch, which is the longest in the world. And, of course, we had to tour the island fort, set way up high on the bluffs, and watch a demonstration of the old cannons and muskets.

So, the days of that week were pretty full. Chris and Lisa were leaving late one night, to try to avoid heavy traffic. That last evening they were there, we had more company over—Kellers, Denals, and a bunch of people from church—and took everybody out in the *Regal* for a cruise-supper. We dropped anchor over by Marquette Bay and watched the sunset. Everybody was awfully quiet as we watched Venus, the first star, come twinkling out while the orange pink clouds were still darkening over our heads.

Waves lapped at the sides of the *Regal,* and she rocked gently to the same rhythm. Over on the shore of Birch Island, a mourning dove started a soft, evening cooing. I stood at the bow, watching the colors change. The sun's last path across the water struck a range from brilliant orange and bright copper to blood red and black where rocks and islands created shadows of varying sizes. Here and there a single tree stood out from the dark bulk of the shoreline, creating a stark, black skeleton against the brilliance.

I kept quiet and listened to everybody ooh and ahh over the scenery. It was beautiful, but sometimes it takes somebody else's fussing over it to make me realize how lucky I am to live where we do. When you see it every day, you quit thinking about it a lot.

It took a while before it registered with me that Mike was standing just behind me, off to one side. I turned a little to see what he was doing but was surprised to see that he was just staring out at the water, too. He hadn't been paying any attention to me at all until he saw me turn. Even then, he just shifted his feet a little, glanced at me, and leaned a hip against the railing. I looked back at the water and wondered what he was thinking about.

"Do you have any lakes like this in California?" I thought maybe he was wishing he was back there.

"Just the ocean. It's a lot bigger."

"Hmm." I wondered if he was going to try to start an argument.

"But it's different."

I looked his way for a second but didn't respond.

"This makes you feel like you're somewhere about three hundred years before now. It's like it's still half-wild."

"Yeah." I leaned over and retrieved the mooring rope that had begun to slip toward the water. "Are you still sorry you moved here?"

"I dunno." Mike shrugged off the question. He was quiet for so long that I didn't think he was going to say anymore. But then he leaned back against the railing more and looked straight at me.

"It's not the place that I think about so much now. It's your bunch. I still think you're kind of weird, you know."

There wasn't much to say to that; so I didn't try to make something up.

"Are your parents the same way?"

"What way?" I knew what he meant, but I figured I might as well make him say it.

He turned away from me again. "Churchy."

I almost snickered but caught myself just in time. "Yeah, I guess they are. But it's more than being churchy, Mike."

He just shrugged again.

"What do you believe about God?" I asked. I was genuinely curious.

"We never thought much about it. Never went to church before here."

I played with the rope in my hands. "Maybe God brought you here so you would think about it."

Another shrug. This would never do, I realized. I felt like shrugging myself and forgetting the whole thing, but something inside poked me again. "Do you know what it means to be a Christian, Mike?"

"I heard your pastor talking about it. I understood it, but I'm just not sure I believe all of it. I still think you guys are weird."

I threw the rope down. Folding my arms on the rail, I stared down at the water. "Well, it's all true. But I can't talk you into having faith. If you really want to know what to believe, you'll have to read the Bible for yourself, I guess, and listen to pastor's messages."

"What about the Bible?" I hadn't heard Mr. Keller coming up behind us. I didn't answer and neither did Mike. He didn't seem to notice but just swung right into another topic. "Well, speaking of Scripture, look at that sunset! Can either of you boys think of what Scripture might say to that scene?" He gestured out at the water.

I could see Mike's face twist in a frown as Mr. Keller went on, talking almost as much to himself as to us.

"The heavens declare the glory of God . . . day unto day uttereth speech, and night unto night sheweth knowledge—"

Mike suddenly spun around and stalked toward the back of the boat. I wasn't sure what to make of that until Mr. Keller leaned against the rail. "He must have a lot on his mind. Keep praying for him, Jeff. I think he's closer to getting saved than he'd like for us to think."

Suddenly I remembered Phil's words from weeks ago: *If God answered prayers for a dog, He won't forget prayers for Mike.* I bowed my head. Maybe that was why God had brought Scout in the first place. I had never really prayed as desperately as I had prayed for Scout. For the first time in my life I had been helpless to do anything *but* pray. Maybe God had been getting me ready to pray for Mike.

I was sorry when Phil started the powerful engine and pointed us toward home. It was starting to seem like one of those nights when nothing could go wrong.

Chapter Thirteen
Nighttime Prowler

I didn't waste any time getting to bed when we reached home. I was tired—the kind of tired that makes you feel dizzy. I mumbled a few goodbyes to our company and stumbled upstairs, not even taking time to brush my teeth before crawling under the covers. Sleep was as close to immediate as sleep could be.

It didn't seem but about two minutes later that I opened my eyes again. I was still tired and groggy, and I couldn't figure out what had dragged me awake. Then I realized that Scout was standing in the middle of the room, stiff and alert. White moonlight from the open window was flooding over him, and I could see the hair on his back standing up. A long, very quiet growl came from him.

A not-so-nice feeling came over me. I strained my ears but couldn't hear anything except the whippoorwill. Very, very slowly and very, very quietly, Scout moved toward the door. He seemed to be floating almost, because not even his nails clicked on the hardwood floor. He growled again, hardly more than a breathy sound.

I was ready to yell for Phil, but Scout saved me the trouble.

The second his nose touched the crack between the door and the doorframe, he exploded. You couldn't have called it a bark. It was more of a roar as he threw himself against the door with an impact that I could feel on the opposite wall. Leaping and scratching, he hurled himself at it again and again, yelling an uninterrupted challenge.

I heard Phil's feet hit the floor in the next room, and now I didn't hesitate to yell. "Phil!" I yelled. "Phil!"

I don't know what I expected him to do, until I heard him yell back.

"Let him out, Jeff!" I guessed that he was groping for his clothes or something; so I bounced from the bed and ran for the door of my room. As I did, I heard a crash downstairs. My heart jumped into my throat, but Scout nearly went crazy.

The crash was followed almost immediately by the bang of the screen door in the living room. I reached the door and pulled it open. I'm pretty sure that it didn't take Scout five jumps to be on the first floor. I could hear him tear through the front room and hit the screen door. A scrabble of toenails on the deck preceded the repeated banging of the loose screen door.

I raced to the window, but in spite of the moon lighting the yard, I couldn't see what he was after, but I was willing to bet somebody had been in the house. We never locked our doors. We never needed to with the army of dogs we keep. Phil ran into the room, feeding shells into the magazine of a rifle as he came. "Where'd he go? What happened?"

"I don't know—he just—" I was interrupted. It sounded like someone had turned loose the Hound of the Baskervilles and all his relatives on our lawn. A man yelled several times, and we heard two shots ring out in quick succession. My pulse froze, but Scout's barking continued. Another yell crescendoed to a scream.

"Call the police." Phil rushed from the room. I could hear his bare feet thumping on the stairs as I ran for the phone in the hall. Jennifer was already there.

"I've got it," she said, "But, Jeff, don't go out—"

I hardly heard her. I was down the stairs after Phil before she could finish. Coming out on the front deck, I was stopped by Phil's harsh voice.

"Stay put! I can't see what he's after."

We both stood by the door, in the shadow from the overhanging roof. We could see Scout by the very edge of the lawn, far down toward the lake. He was stationed at the bottom of a young maple tree, leaping into the air over and over, sinking his teeth into the soft bark of the tree and tearing it off in vain attempts to reach whatever was up there. His constant, yelling barks sounded like the wild, brawling challenge that you hear on crime shows from the junkyard security dogs: A-rur-ah! A-rur-ah! A-rur-ah!

He had gone crazy, I thought. "Phil, let's go see," I said, moving forward slightly. He clamped on my arm with an iron grip.

"Don't you move. He might still have the gun."

"Who?" I wondered how he knew somebody was down there.

141

"Whoever was in the house. I could hear him. You were probably too close to Scout's commotion, but I could hear his footsteps when he ran out."

We waited and waited and waited. I felt like I was someone else, watching a crazy scene from a detective show. Everything was dead silent except for Scout's furious barking. I'll tell you one thing, though, I sure didn't feel tired anymore.

Sometime during the wait, Jennifer came to the screen door right behind us. "Phil?" she whispered.

"Yeah, we're right here." His voice was almost as low as hers.

"I can't find anything missing in here. The toaster was knocked off the stand by the kitchen door, but nothing else looks like it's been touched."

"You didn't touch anything yourself, did you?"

"No."

Finally, we heard the wail of approaching sirens. All three of us breathed a sigh of relief. Then, something brushed against my foot. I almost screamed. I did jump, and that made Jennifer yelp, although she was still inside the door.

Looking down, I realized that it was Chops. She acted funny, though. I stooped down to pick her up, and she whined. "What's the matter, girl?" I said in a whisper.

Her whine turned into a cough, and she started to gag. I could feel her heaving and shuddering in my arms. "She's sick!" I exclaimed. Jennifer opened the door a crack and reached for her.

"Give her here. I'll take her into the kitchen and see what's wrong."

Then I started wondering about Reefer and Candy. I guess my brain was a little slow on the draw just then, because it began to occur to me that they should have been here from the very first, raising all crazy commotion out on the lawn with Scout. There wasn't a lot of time to wonder, though, because all of a sudden, there was a lot of noise and people around. Mr. Curtis, our county sheriff, and several state policemen were coming around the house, with huge search-beam flashlights.

They started asking questions. Phil identified himself and answered them faster than I could really follow what was going on. The front yard-lights were clicked on, and the lawn was illuminated nearly all the way to the lake.

We could see Scout clearly now. His challenging barks hadn't abated one bit, although he had stopped leaping at the tree. He was standing, partly crouched, as though ready to spring on a fraction of a second's notice.

The policemen fanned out and began approaching the tree. I held my breath as they moved, braced to hear more shots. None came. They reached the tree and shone their big lights up into it. Even we could make out the figure of a man perched among the lower branches.

Mr. Curtis moved closer to Scout. We could hear his voice as he spoke to him but couldn't hear what he said. Scout ignored him anyway. Mr. Curtis reached out and took his collar. I gasped as I saw a lightning snap and a flash of teeth. I don't think Scout meant to bite him or he wouldn't have missed, but he made his point. Mr. Curtis didn't touch him again.

Scout was leaping at the trunk of the tree again, in obvious attempts to reach the man he had cornered. His barks almost drowned out Mr. Curtis's call.

"Wingate! Come get your dog!"

"Call him, Jeff," Phil ordered quickly.

I hadn't realized how dry my mouth was. When I yelled for Scout, only a croak came out. I pursed my lips and whistled, then tried again. "Scout! Come!" Better this time, I thought.

Scout, however, ignored me completely. That had never happened before. I repeated my order, but it fell on deaf ears.

"Come and get him!" the call from the lawn was repeated. "The man's unarmed!"

Phil ejected the shells from his rifle and laid it down, and we both made our way down the hill. "Scout!" I called as I came up to him, "Stop that racket! Come here! Scout!" I was getting mad. He had never disobeyed like this before. I went to him and grabbed his collar, jerking it hard.

"Scout! Quiet!" He still ignored me and tried to pull away. I was jerked to my knees with the effort it took to keep a hold on his collar. Phil came up and joined me. Between the two of us, we literally dragged him away from the tree.

It was as though he'd really gone insane. He fought and struggled and barked and snarled until our dragging on the chain collar cut off his breath. Then he choked and began gasping out his barks as though he was being strangled.

We continued to hold him as the police brought the man down from the tree. Not till he was full in the light of their flashes did Phil and I both recognize him.

145

He was our nosy friend from the day of the Moran horse show.

"Well! Hello again." Phil's voice was cold and sarcastic.

"You know him?" The sergeant was surprised.

"He was hanging around Jeff and Randy Keller, a couple weeks ago, asking a lot of questions about the dog." Phil took a fresh grip on Scout's collar, who seemed to be willing to hang himself to get his teeth into the stranger. "I don't know what he wanted, though; Jen checked through the house, and there doesn't seem to be anything missing."

"That's right." An officer came up behind us. "There isn't. At least not that we can find—unless he's got something on him."

"Nope," another said. They had just completed a real professional-like frisk on the stranger, who had yet to say a word. "But I think that dog is nuts. Look at him!" Everyone did.

Not for an instant had he ceased attempting to get to the captured man. "It is odd." Phil's voice was puzzled. "He never disobeys. Well, me, maybe, but not Jeff. It's enough to make me wonder where he's run into this guy before—hey!"

The officer who had frisked the man was now jerking his hands behind him to handcuff him, while another officer began reading him his rights. As his hands went behind his back, his jacket opened in the front. At Phil's exclamation, I looked toward him and saw the red foam-rubber tube jammed in his belt.

"The tube!" I yelled.

Mr. Curtis looked from us to the captive. "Tube?" he asked.

"The red tube in his belt!" Phil almost let go of Scout in his excitement. "That's what he took out of the house!"

"This?" The officer frowned in disbelief as he went and took the tube from the man. "You have to be kidding!"

"No, we're not." I turned loose of Scout, ran to the man, and took the tube. "Watch!" I ran back to the still-struggling Scout, dropped the tube in front of him, and spoke sharply, "Scout, down! Quiet."

The resulting silence made our ears ring. Scout dropped to the ground, crouching protectively over the small, red object.

"For pete's sake, what is it?" the officer holding the captive asked in obvious amazement. "That's what all the commotion was over?"

"We don't know what it is." Phil was rubbing his hands together to restore their circulation after the ordeal on Scout's collar. "Scout found it out where we found him a couple months ago. He's in love with it, I guess." Phil rapidly outlined the whole story for the benefit of the officers who hadn't heard it before.

When he had finished, one of the state policemen came close to us with a strange look on his face. "Can you get it from him? I'd like to look at it."

"Sure." I reached down under Scout's chin. "Stay," I told him, while I picked up the tube and handed it to Mr. Curtis. Scout watched with his usual concern, but he didn't move.

The policeman inspected the tube carefully. After a long moment, he turned to Phil. "I'm going to need to take this with me. There's something I need to check out—if I'm wrong, I'll bring it back, but either way, it'll be used as evidence against this guy." He indicated the silent captive with a jerk of his head.

"All right." Phil didn't ask any questions, and I took my cue from him, although I was bursting with curiosity.

I was feeling awfully tired all of a sudden. It seemed like it took forever for the police to get their statements about exactly what had happened. We all made our way back to the house and around to the driveway.

"Oh, Phil," the sheriff said, "I almost forgot. Your wife took the little dog to the vet. It was really sick I guess, and she figured you'd be tied up for quite a while."

"She did? Hey," Phil exclaimed for the second time that night, "where are Reefer and Candy?" In all the hubbub, I guess it was the first time it had occurred to him too. I'd kind of forgotten it again myself, since the police had arrived. Scout had been making enough noise for all three of them anyway.

The state police were leaving already, but the sheriff came back. "You mean your other big dog? And the setter? I thought maybe you had them shut away somewhere."

I was worried, now, and the sheriff's next remark didn't ease my mind any.

"The little dog was acting really strange. I wonder—"

"Jake?" I was barely in time to catch Phil's glance in my direction as he questioned the sheriff.

"What's happened to them?" I asked, my voice catching in my throat.

"We don't know, Jeff," Phil said quietly. "Why don't you go inside and call the vet. Talk to Jennifer and see what's going on. Leave Scout out here, and we'll take a look around for them."

I opened my mouth to protest, but Phil shook his head at me.

"Go on, Jeff. Now." I did.

Dr. Anderson himself answered the phone; so I asked him what was the matter with Chops.

"She's eaten something that made her sick, Jeff. She'll be all right, I'm sure, but I haven't rightly figured out what it was though. Jennifer's told me what's been going on down there—so I'm thinking it's likely that your trespasser gave it to her."

A cold hand grabbed my heart and squeezed. "Something to make her sick?" I asked. "Like to kill her?"

There was a long hesitation on the other end of the line. "Maybe. But like I said, I can't tell for sure. She didn't get much of it, if that's what it was. It could have been some kind of a poison. A professional thief will do that sometimes, if he knows there's a watchdog around. Where are your other monsters? Are they all okay?"

Very faintly, I heard a short, sharp bark from Scout, as though they were way out by the road. "I don't know. Phil's looking for them. They haven't been around." My voice was almost too thick to fit through my throat. I could feel tears of fear pricking at my eyelids.

Dr. Anderson's silence was unbroken this time. I forced myself to ask him what I needed to. I just wanted to get off the phone and find out what was happening outside. "When's Jennifer coming home?"

"I'll be able to send Chops with her in half an hour or so."

"Yeah," I gulped. "Phil will probably want her to call before she leaves so we'll know when to expect her."

After all, it was about four o'clock in the morning. I replaced the receiver, went to the pantry, and rummaged for a flashlight. But before I found one, I heard Phil coming back. The sheriff's car started, and I could hear it moving down the drive.

I listened for the sound of three sets of toenails scrabbling on the deck as Phil clumped across, but all I heard was one. Scout followed Phil into the kitchen alone.

Phil didn't have to tell me. I knew by the look on his face.

"They're dead, aren't they?" I felt the tears escape my eyes and start down my cheeks.

He nodded. "The guy must have poisoned them, Jeff." I realized that Phil was about to cry himself. "He must have really meant business about sneaking in here. I don't know—I didn't even hear them bark. Maybe he just hung around down by the end of the driveway until they went to investigate. They're right down there in the woods. I think maybe he thought he'd gotten Scout, or I don't think he ever would have dared come into the house."

Phil sat down heavily in a chair at the table. "The sheriff's going to take them away and see if they can determine what it was."

I took an angry swipe at the tears and gave my attention to Scout. He kept nudging my hand, and absently, I kept stroking him. "They almost got Chops, too," I said. "Dr. Anderson guessed that somebody had tried to poison her."

Much, much later, I was finally back in bed. A grayish, foggy dawn was breaking over the channels as

150

I fought to banish the thoughts that kept marching through my head and get back to sleep.

Reefer and Candy! I thought. You poor things! How are we ever going to tell Mom and Dad? Could we have prevented this if we'd reported the red tube? I cringed as I remembered how easily we had all dismissed the possibility that it was important.

I rolled over, pressing my cheek against the cold, smooth sheet, and looked down at Scout. He lay in his customary spot on the rug, but he was looking up at me intently, ears perked.

"I sure do wish you could talk, dog."

Chapter Fourteen

The Day Things Went Wrong

I slept late the next morning. When I finally made it downstairs, it was nearly noon. Jennifer tried to get me to eat something, but I really wasn't hungry.

"Where's Phil?" I wasn't sure I wanted to know, but I asked anyway.

"He got a call from the sheriff a couple hours ago, Jeff." She was sort of avoiding my eyes. "I'm not sure what it was all about, but they asked him to go into St. Ignace. He said he'd call when he found out what was going on."

I watched Scout as he investigated around under the table for some stray crumbs. "Jennifer, do you think this means they're going to find Scout's real owner? That guy must have known what the tube was."

"You know that I can't guess that any better than you." She shut the refrigerator door and leaned back against it, looking me over thoroughly. "Are you sure you don't want some breakfast?"

"No, I'm not hungry. I just wish I knew what was going on, and I wish I knew how we're going to explain to Mom and Dad about Reefer and Candy."

SCOUT

"They'll understand, Jeff." Silence reigned in the kitchen for a few moments. All I could hear was a big fly buzzing against the outside of the window screen over the sink. Jennifer spoke again, this time with a lot of hesitation.

"Jeff, um, it does seem likely that with everything that happened last night that they're going to be able to establish some kind of a link to Scout's past."

I didn't answer her. Scout tired of his search for tidbits, coming to rest his head on my knee.

"We've always known he must be a valuable dog. It wouldn't be right if every effort wasn't made to find out where he came from. What if he had belonged to you in the first place, Jeff? Wouldn't you want someone to make every effort to try to find you?"

"Yeah." It made sense when she said it like that, but I still didn't feel like celebrating.

"Oh, Jeff." She pulled out a chair and sat down. "I know this is hard on you. But it's just another thing in your life that God is going to use to make you grow into the person He wants you to be. Just like with Mike, when you figured you would rather die than try to make friends with him."

I looked up quickly. "I never said that."

"You thought it, though, didn't you?"

I looked down. I didn't need to answer her.

"That worked out all right. Things are a lot better now than they were before."

She was right, but I still couldn't see how the possibility of losing Scout was going to improve anything.

"You need to think a lot about Romans 8:28 today, Jeff. 'All things work together for good to them that

154

love God, to them who are the called according to his purpose.' You may not understand, but you have to trust God anyway and keep your attitude right meanwhile."

I nodded, but I'd had about all I could take just then. I was afraid I was going to do something silly if the conversation went any further. The backs of my eyes were already itchy.

"I guess I'm going to go out for a walk." I got up to leave.

"You really should eat something."

"I said I'm not hungry!" Before I could even think, the tension in me just leaped however it could. Before I'd even finished, I was ashamed. I didn't need Jennifer's quiet reminder.

"I'm as sorry about all this as you are, Jeff. Please don't yell at me or anyone else just because you can't change the way things are."

I couldn't even make myself say I was sorry, even though I was. I just snapped my fingers to Scout and walked out of the kitchen.

It was going to be a hot, humid day. There was only the least little breeze on the beach. Scout paced close beside me as I trudged aimlessly through the sand. He must have known something was bothering me, because usually he would be bounding in and out of the woods, inspecting everything we passed.

We hadn't gotten much more than a quarter mile up the beach when I heard a shrill whistle from back toward the house. It was Phil. I knew that, and suddenly I knew more than that. I fought the urge to run for the woods, Scout at my heels. The big Doberman stood looking up at me quizzically. He knew the summons too, and he couldn't figure out the way I was acting.

I felt like I was moving in a dream as I turned and retraced my steps back to the house. I dropped my hand on the head of the dog who stalked beside me like a personal guard. The break in the trees to the east of our dock came closer and closer. The wind was blowing in our face, and I felt Scout stiffen before I saw that his ears were pricked.

As we came around the last of the trees before our yard, I stopped. Scout stopped too—and stood still as a rock. Quivering and tense, he stretched his muzzle ahead as though he could bridge the hundred yards separating him from the figures that stood by the front deck.

I saw him drop to a crouch, a trembling whine rising from his throat. A lurch, a spray of sand against the cuff of my jeans, and he was gone: flying up the hill, howling in a constant, frantic crescendo. I saw the tall uniformed figure that stood between Phil and Jennifer take a step forward, but I turned away the second before Scout's flying rush joined the two together.

Scout's yips and howls of delight followed me, along with the man's fainter exclamations, as I went out on the dock, climbed into the *Luau,* untied her, and pushed off. I wanted no part of the reunion. I was terribly afraid that I was going to be sick to my stomach. I started the motor and headed toward Hessel Bay, but my actions were just as mechanical and pointless as my walk had been a few minutes before. I'm not sure where all I went before I found myself drifting out on the far side of Government Island. I watched the waves crashing off the rough shoreline. My wandering gaze picked out a small hollow in the steep embankment, up toward the point.

Had it really only been, what, ten weeks? No more than that, I realized with a start. It seemed like eternity. I've never been much for wishing for things that I knew I couldn't have, but I found myself wishing for any part of the summer back again, at any cost. It didn't really hit me until that moment that I'd never really thought I would have to give Scout up.

A lot of hours must have gone by, because the sun was far toward the west when I docked the *Luau* at our pier again. Somewhere at the back of my mind, I recognized the possibility that Phil was going to be angry with me. Not until I climbed up on the dock did I realize that he was sitting on the deck of the *Regal*. I didn't say anything but just stopped to check the *Luau*'s mooring again.

"Are you ready to talk to him?" Phil's voice wasn't angry. He dropped lightly to the dock.

"Not particularly, but I guess it doesn't matter." Phil didn't answer right away. He looked up toward the house, then down, scuffing his toe against the rough dock planking.

"He's a military man, Jeff. An officer. Lieutenant Grady is his name."

I stuffed my hands in my pockets and hunched my shoulders, wanting to hear, but not wanting to hear.

"You know what the Special Forces branch of the army is, Jeff?"

"Sort of."

"Well, they're a specially trained group that does a lot of hard, high-risk things. Some of them work with K-9 units as well, and that's where Scout came in. I want the lieutenant to tell you the whole story, but they'd thought Scout to be dead until, well, until the police found that tube."

"It wasn't just a training device, then?"

"No."

"Do I have to talk to him, Phil? I know he's going to take Scout—I just don't want to have to even know what he looks like."

"Yes, you have to talk to him, Jeff. You're not going to be cowardly about this. And I don't think he has any choice but to take Scout. It's probably not his decision to make."

I swallowed the lump in my throat and nodded. Slowly, we made our way up the long, sloping lawn to the house. Our steps made an unusual amount of noise on the wooden deck as we crossed to the door. A wet, inquisitive nose met me as the door opened. "Hi, boy." I rubbed his ears before stepping the rest of the way through the door to face the man that stood up from the sofa.

He was tall, taller than Phil by far. His hair was dark, a perfect match for the eyes that met mine with a frank honesty that I almost couldn't stand. The uniform was impressive. I didn't know what all the stripes, bars, and ribbons meant, but I figured he hadn't got them by hanging back when things got tough.

"Hello, Jeff," he said quietly, stepping forward and extending his hand.

"Hi." I couldn't think of anything else to say; so I shook his hand quickly and turned my attention back to Scout. The big dog was restless, pacing back and forth from the man to me.

"Your brother has told me a lot about what's been going on this summer."

"Yeah." I wasn't intentionally being rude. I just wasn't sure what to do or say. I think it would have been easier if the guy had been nasty, or stuck up. I could have disliked him then and had an excuse for all the hostility I was feeling.

"I thought maybe you'd like to hear how he came to be here." The lieutenant's gaze hadn't wavered one bit from me. I couldn't deny my interest in that story.

"Yes, sir." I fumbled for what seemed like proper language for this man. "I guess I would."

"Good." Lieutenant Grady seemed almost relieved. "I've already sketched in the details for your brother and sister-in-law, but I figured I'd tell you all the whole story at one time." He moved back to his seat on the couch, beckoning for me to sit down.

I did but chose a chair instead of the couch where he was. Phil and Jennifer settled themselves down, too. Scout flopped in his usual spot on the rug in the middle of the room.

Lieutenant Grady looked at him briefly and grinned. "You've been good to him—he feels right at home."

None of us answered; so he launched into his story. "I've worked with the K-9 units for almost ten years, now. I'm a little bit limited in what I can tell you about exactly what I do. Since the K-9s have been incorporated into a particular branch of the U.S. Special Forces, I've been working with them on some test projects, to see just how well they were going to work out for particular jobs.

"One day, a little over two years ago, a new dog was assigned to our unit, fresh out of what you might call 'basic training.' He'd actually been discarded as a routine K-9 candidate because of his size. They have certain size limits, as well as requirements. The trainers felt that he had so much potential though, that they'd thought maybe we'd have some use for him, since we work outside regular channels so much." The lieutenant paused for a long time, settled back on the sofa, and looked at Scout.

"So there was Scout—hardly more than a big, gangly puppy—just over a year old. I worked with him a little bit and decided that he was a wonder-dog. Of all the animals I'd ever worked with, he was, by far, superior, whether you're talking about strength, smarts, speed, or whatever. I poured everything I'd learned into making him the finest dog possible. We were doing some experimenting during that time with a new type of courier device: a fairly small, foam-rubber tube. It was part of a trial to see what kind of part the dogs could play in things. A large part of their training centered on the tubes. The tubes varied in color, depending on what they were being used for, but all of them had a small hollow in the middle that was filled with a plastic type of microfilm."

Lieutenant Grady leaned down and picked up the briefcase that stood by the couch. Snapping the locks open, he extracted three familiar looking tubes, one red, one green, and one orange. Scout pricked up his ears at the sight of them.

"How do you get them open?" I asked. "We tried and tried to figure out what it was."

"They don't come apart. The only way to get to the film is to cut it apart—and they're purposely made pretty tough. See, the tube is created especially for its own certain piece of film—it's sealed in the middle. This is all still pretty much in the experimental stages, but that's about all I can tell you."

"Now, as far as the dogs are concerned, they're taught that guarding, retrieving, or whatever, when it has to do with those tubes, is Priority One, so to speak. The tubes also give off a very strong scent to the dogs; so they can find them at a greater distance by scent than a human could by sight."

Bit by bit, as the man talked, the story began to fall together for me.

"Last June, I was on a special assignment. Sort of what you might call undercover. Another man from my patrol and I were in charge of delivering some highly confidential information to another place—I'm sorry I can't tell you much more about that—but part of our "cover" was to pass through this area, ostensibly as tourists. We were on a large yacht. Just the two of us. What I didn't know was that my partner had turned traitor. He had sold out to a scheme of stealing the tube and the material that it contained. Early one morning, just after we'd left the Cedarville Bay, he made his move. It was supposed to look like an outside job, of course, and not be connected with him in any way. Apparently, another boat was supposed to meet us, before we got out into open water, and take the tube. When they tried to board our boat, there was a terrific struggle. I was able to get to the radio and yell for help, but I was injured quite badly and knocked out in the process. It was several days before I came to, and by then I was back at my base in Georgia. We'd been picked up by a military hydro-jet. My "partner" reported that Scout had been shot and dumped overboard by the other men—which wasn't actually too far from the truth. They just hadn't used a gun for fear of alerting someone to trouble."

"You mean they tried to kill him with something else?" I knew I shouldn't interrupt, but I couldn't believe my ears.

"Yes. A knife, from the description your vet gave of the wounds and the looks of the scars on him. If I know anything about Scout, he knew that his job was to keep that tube with me. He probably could have saved himself from any danger if he'd been willing to abandon it. As it was, the men probably cut him up, figuring he'd bleed to death, and either crowded or outright threw him overboard."

Jennifer looked a little sick. "How did your partner explain all this?" She was as puzzled as the rest of us.

"He said that the men had escaped with the tube. As nearly as we can figure, I was supposed to have been killed, too, but in the scramble, I got to the radio, and Scout got to the tube—neither of which my "partner" had counted on. That's what started his headaches. Scout was trying to keep the tube during part of the fight, and what with all the scuffling, it was apparently lost overboard. The dirty skunk of a partner kept the whole story as quiet and messed up as he could, while the outside fellow, after hearing later this summer about your family finding Scout, tried to discover if the tube was still around."

Phil spoke for the first time since the story had begun. "Jeff must have found him not too long afterwards, that same morning."

"Yes. I expect he'd have bled to death if it had been much longer."

Lieutenant Grady leaned forward and stretched a little. "The rest of the story you know better than I, except that the man who broke into your home last night is the same one who jumped us on the boat last June."

Everyone was quiet for quite a while. Jennifer was the first to break the silence. "He really is a very special dog, then."

"He's as special as they come." The lieutenant's voice showed his affection for Scout. "Last night, one of the police officers suspected that the tube might be more important than it looked. They cut into it, and once they found the film, it didn't take long to get it into the proper hands."

"Why didn't they get a report on this before when they made inquiries about it two months ago?" Phil looked a little irritated. "We suspected then that the dog might be from the military, but they said no."

The lieutenant frowned. "That's one of the downfalls of red tape and dishonesty combined. It's very involved to make any kind of inquiry about my branch of the service at all, because it's all highly classified information. Plus, my crooked partner, who, technically, had been in charge of the operation, apparently managed to intercept the inquiry. We know that, even though we haven't figured out all the details yet. Would you believe it wasn't until last night, when the film was actually back in the originator's hands, that my ratty partner's scheme was even uncovered? He's in custody now, waiting for a court-martial. It'll go pretty hard on him, but I wasn't even concerned. I commandeered a pilot within the hour, and we were on our way up here."

"They have a little plane up at the Hessel strip, Jeff," Phil told me. "There are a few loose ends to wrap up, but they're going to be leaving tomorrow night."

I nodded. I didn't trust myself to say anything. There was a baseball-sized lump in my throat.

Lieutenant Grady's face was grave. "I have to confess, Jeff, that I'm kind of at a loss for something to say to you. If this had lasted a week or two, it would have been easier for you, but here it's been more than two months. I know how I would feel if I were you, but, well, Scout is property of the United States government—he doesn't even belong to me."

"I know." I choked out the words and stood up. I didn't want him to say anything more. I wasn't even sure what I was feeling—anger maybe—but I knew that I wanted out of that room. Scout got up and came to me, whining anxiously and sticking a cold nose into my hand.

"I'm amazed at how well he's taken to you, Jeff. Never before was he anything more than a one-person dog."

"It's been the same way here, this summer," Phil cut in quietly, "except that the one person was Jeff."

"Yes." Lieutenant Grady shook his head in wonder. "Your brother has told me about some of your experiences this summer, Jeff—and I think Scout can always be proud of his new scars."

I nodded silently again. Then suddenly words came out in a rush. "Look, I'm going to go for a ride, I think. Is he staying here tonight, or do you have to take him?"

"I'm afraid I have to take him tonight, but we'll both be back tomorrow for a little while before we leave for Georgia."

I nodded. With a quick pat on Scout's head, I spun for the door. "Jeff—" Jennifer's concerned voice followed me.

"Let him go." I heard Phil's quiet response as the screen door bounced shut behind me.

Chapter Fifteen
Scout's Choice

The night brought heavy thunderstorms. I lay in bed, awake most of the night for the second night in a row. I listened to the torrents of rain that poured over our house, the wind that tossed the big trees around, and the crashes and rumbles of the thunder and lightning. I drifted off to sleep every now and then, but my only dreams were of Scout being taken away from me by men in uniforms, his big dark eyes fixed on me, pleading with me to do something.

Toward morning, the storm blew itself out and the temperature rose. That brought a heavy fog rising off the water. The rain returned throughout the day to drizzle a little bit, but that suited my mood pretty well. I didn't do much, unless you count helping Jennifer roll out the pie dough. Phil had gone back up to Bay City Lake and retrieved the containers of berries the day before. They were a little extra ripe, but not spoiled, and that never hurts anything with blueberry pie or ice cream.

Mostly, I thought of ways to try to talk the lieutenant into leaving Scout with me, but even while I did, I knew that it was right for him to go. If I had lost him like that, I would take him back. When I could drag my mind off Scout and Lieutenant Grady, I kept wondering how we were going to explain to Mom and Dad about Reefer and Candy. Jennifer still didn't expect it would be a problem.

"They'll understand, Jeff," she repeated, going out of her way to try to make me feel better about everything. "They're not going to hold anybody responsible."

"I think Dad will. He'll say that we should have checked every possibility—used our heads. Phil did want to give it to the police when I first found it, but I was the one that talked him out of it."

"If he'd really thought it was important, Jeff, he wouldn't have let you talk him out of it."

I hoped she was right, but I had my doubts. When lunch came, all three of us sat around the table and poked at our food. Homemade stew had never seemed so unappetizing to me before. For once, Jennifer didn't try to talk anybody into eating. Not even herself. After lunch, Jennifer curled up with a book, and Phil disappeared into his room with his lexicon and Greek New Testament. Because he taught a few Bible courses, he liked to keep up on his Greek. I wondered if in his studies he would find some reason for all of this—maybe that was what he was looking for.

I walked out to visit the horses, walked down and sat on the dock, went up and sat in my room—it was one of those kinds of days, you know? We were all just waiting for the lieutenant to come back with Scout. By this time, I wasn't even sure if it was going to be best for me to see him again. It sure wasn't going to be any easier to say goodbye. Nobody said anything about supper, and the afternoon stretched toward evening. Finally Phil came out and said, "Well, nobody's been on Repeat today. I guess I'll go take her out for a little bit. Anybody want to come?"

Jennifer and I both shook our heads. I went out and sat on the deck to wait. It couldn't possibly be much longer. I was busy thinking that Mom and Dad wouldn't even get to see him when I heard a scrabble of tiny toenails and watched Chops scramble up the stairs to the deck. She came to the side of my chair and whined. "Hi, kid," I said. I knew she was lonely and puzzled. "How ya feeling?"

She leaped into my lap and tried to lick my face, still whining. "Thanks, but no thanks." I pushed her down into a sitting position. "You'd better get used to it, kid. You're going to be an only dog for a while. Unless Mom decides we need some more."

That was a probability, I knew. I could hardly remember a time when we hadn't had at least three or four. My thoughts were jerked off that subject by the crunch of wheels on the gravel out front. Chops hurled herself off my lap, off the deck, and disappeared around the corner, yapping for all she was worth. I braced myself for the knock on the kitchen door and Jennifer's response.

"Oh, hello." Her voice sounded surprised. "Won't you come in? I'm Jennifer Wingate."

"Sergeant Rallen, ma'am. Thank you. Has Lieutenant Grady returned yet?"

"No. I rather thought that you were he."

"I see. Would you mind if I waited for him? He should be along any minute."

"Of course not. Have a seat. My husband should be back shortly. He'll have heard your car."

There was a momentary silence. Then Jennifer spoke again. "Where is the lieutenant? We had expected him back before now."

"He's, ah, well, doing some final checking on what to do about things."

"What to do?" To my surprise I detected just a faint note of irritation in Jennifer's normally quiet voice. "Sir, Jeff knows he can't keep the dog. Waiting is not making it easier for any of us."

I didn't want to hear any more of this conversation. Carefully, I got up and made my way off the deck. I went down to the beach and started aimlessly walking. I didn't really mean to go far, but after several cuts in and out of the woods, I realized I was almost up to the bay.

What do you think you're doing? I asked myself angrily. Delaying anything? What if he comes while you're gone? You might not get to see him at all.

Still, I went up to where the sand climbed into partly grassy hills and dunes, and I sat down facing the water. The fog was lifting and the rain had stopped, but the sand was still wet. I could feel it soaking into my jeans as I sat there. A breeze sprang up, washing the beach in the smell of wet cedar and spurce from the nearby trees. I rested my chin on my arms and watched the waves crashing on the beach. They were coming higher and higher every minute, and growing rougher and rougher with the wind. I watched their rhythm until I was nearly too entranced to hear the soft plop of approaching footsteps. I jerked my head up. Lieutenant Grady and Scout were approaching. Scout bounded

from the man's side, raced to me, and nearly bowled me over with his greeting. "Hi, dog," I muttered as I roughed up his ears. He groaned a little and fell over, front end first, in the sand. Rolling on his back, he grabbed my arm in his teeth. I avoided looking at the lieutenant until he spoke to me.

"Hello, Jeff."

"Hi."

"Do you mind if I sit down for a minute? It's been a long day."

"No—I mean, go ahead." We sat there in silence for a few minutes. I could tell that the sun was getting low. What was left of the fog was growing darker. A loud blast of a foghorn out on the lake made us both jump a little. He chuckled, but I concentrated on finding the outline of the big freighter in the dusky light. It was easier than facing him.

"Jeff, there's something we have to talk about."

"What?"

"Scout, of course."

I knew that, I wanted to say. But what about him?

"I spent quite a bit of time talking with my superiors today, after we got everything else wound up here. They reminded me of something I had not exactly forgotten, but something I just hadn't been thinking about."

He paused for another long time, watching the sea gulls soar around us.

"Jeff, Scout is a very special dog. You know that. He's worth thousands and thousands of dollars to the United States. Maybe you couldn't even put a price tag on the man-hours and expertise that've gone into training him." Lieutenant Grady sighed. "On top of that, he's one in a million to me, Jeff. Just like he is to you.

You know that I came up here for the express purpose of taking him back with me?"

I nodded. That was pretty obvious. "He belongs to you, sir. As much as I hate it, I know it's right that he goes with you. If he were mine, I'd want him back."

"I appreciate your saying that, Jeff, but, well, it wasn't until last night that I wondered if I was doing the right thing."

A single butterfly made a mad dash through my stomach, only to disappear at his next words.

"That doesn't mean I'm going to give him to you. He belongs to our base, and he has a very important job to do. The only hitch is, well, he's not going to be worth a red cent down there if he's wishing he were back here. The kind of job he does, well, he has to love it in order to do it well—to do it right. Do you understand what I'm saying?"

"I think so. You're afraid he's going to be pouting down there because he wants to be here with me."

"Exactly. But, Jeff, I'll be honest with you. If there were any way I could force him, I would. But you can't do that with a dog like Scout. It won't work. All we can do is leave the choice up to him."

"How are you planning on doing that? You can't ask him." This was beginning to sound a little ridiculous to me.

"Yes, we can, in a way. He's lying there now, not paying any attention to either of us. In a minute I'm going to get up and walk back to the house. My plane is waiting for me right now, and we have to get off the airstrip before dark; so I have to hurry. Whether or not Scout goes with me is going to be his choice. Don't call him, say anything, do anything, or even really look at him. I'll do the same. If he follows me, he comes. If he stays here with you, you can keep him for good."

My heart started pounding so that I thought I could hear it over the rising wind.

"That way, we'll know what he wants to do." Lieutenant Grady's voice was very quiet. "Either way, Jeff, thank you. For everything you did for him." He extended his hand to me.

I took it, shaking it as firmly as I could manage. "I guess I couldn't have done anything else."

"No, I guess not. Goodbye, Jeff."

"Goodbye, sir."

Not quickly, but very deliberately, he pushed himself up off the sand. I didn't watch him go but fixed my attention on the huge freighter that was drifting toward the Mackinac Straits. Its running lights were glowing faintly through the mist. Scout bounded to his feet and looked at me expectantly.

I looked away from him. He took a couple steps toward Lieutenant Grady, then whirled back to me and whined. When I didn't respond, he leaped back in front of me and gave a half bark. Then he dashed away again, stopping about ten feet from me. He was telling me as plainly as he could that he wanted me to go too. I gripped my hands together around my knees and concentrated on the whitecaps, now that I couldn't see the freighter. I knew that a single finger-snap would glue Scout to his tracks. No one would ever know.

The big Doberman made one last rush in front of me. His bark was full force this time, followed by a whine. He made the short dash away, stopped, and barked again. I gritted my teeth to keep from whispering, "Scout, stay!"

For endless moments he stood there. I watched a flock of sea gulls gathering to my right, and counted to the crash of the waves on the wet sand. "One, two, three, four, five . . ." I was beginning to think eternity had started, but when I reached twenty-one, Scout wheeled and dashed away, tearing up the beach after the disappearing lieutenant. The scratch of his flying paws in the sand gradually faded into nothing.

Tears prickled at the back of my eyes. Stop it! I told myself. At least you know now that he wanted to go. The foghorn blared again, fainter this time. I put my head down on my arms again. I could have called him back. He would have heard me and obeyed. But it would have been wrong, I told myself. I was afraid I would do it anyway. I was afraid Scout would miss me. I was afraid that someone else someday would injure him again—maybe kill him. All the fear and regret crowded my mind, and all I could do was silently struggle out a plea of "Lord, help!" I didn't even know if I was asking for Him to send Scout back to me or to protect Scout or to help me give him up.

The wind really picked up as I sat. Probably, another storm was coming. It grew so loud again that between it and the waves, I could hardly hear the scolding of the nearby gulls until they all rose, thundering away at the same time. Their wild cries were enough to make me lift my head and watch them wing away. As I did so, something cold poked me in the back of the neck.

Yelping in surprise, I bounded to my feet, only to be flattened by a hundred pounds of Doberman pinscher. "Scout!" I yelled, squirming around to see him. He gave an ecstatic growl and attacked my leg.

"Scout, you came back!" I wondered briefly if Lieutenant Grady had sent him back, but at the same time, I knew that he wouldn't have. I didn't have time for any more wondering though, as dozens of new thoughts came alive.

"Hey, dog!" I yelled at him. He attacked my leg, and we went rolling and wrestling through the wet sand, over and over. One on top of the other and vice-versa. "Guess what! Mom and Dad are coming home day after tomorrow! And we've got all the time in the world to see Mike get saved and to love this place, and you're going to get to walk the bridge on Labor Day, and hey! Mutt, have you ever seen snow?"

He began to bark as I kept carrying on like a crazy person. With his barking and my yelling we cleared the beach completely of the gulls. I felt pent-up adrenalin from the last two days streaming through me.

"Come on, dog." I pulled myself up to my feet at last. "I'm starved. Let's go talk Phil into getting us a pizza—and I think there's blueberry pie up there, too."

Scout shook himself free of sand and began to follow me, but suddenly I heard something: the faint buzz of a small airplane. "Hey, that must be—" I interrupted myself by dashing down toward the water. Turning around, I was barely in time to see a small aircraft coming. It hadn't made much height yet, and it looked as though it was barely clearing the trees. I jumped up and down and waved frantically, even though I was pretty sure they wouldn't be able to see me. Maybe or maybe not. The wings dipped from side to side, the lights blinked, and the twin engines whined to a higher pitch as the little plane buzzed over my head.

I turned around, barely noticing that Scout's attention was also fixed on the plane. Side by side we stood, watching the toy-sized figure soar out over the water, gain height, and become nothing but a small point against the darkening sky. Up, up, and it was gone, leaving the beach once again to the crash of the waves and the whistle of the wind.